CELIA'S DREAM

THE EYMANN FAMILY TRILOGY – BOOK 3
AN AMISH ROMANCE

Naomi Troyer

Contents

Chapter 1
Courage From Chicken Fried Steak

As the leaves changed from emerald green to shades of orange and burgundy, Celia could feel the change in herself as well.

This kitchen might be the one she was raised in, the one where she had learned to cook at her mother's side, but it was no longer hers. Just like the living room, the porch, and even her bedroom no longer felt as if she belonged.

Instead, she felt like an intruder.

Celia understood change, probably better than her siblings with certain matters, and just like she understood change, she understood the need to move on.

At twenty-four, Celia felt underfoot, over-appreciated, and placated by her family. She had never had adventures of her own or even attended singings, because for the last few years Celia had focused on her family, and most of all on her mother.

Her mother's Alzheimer's was becoming a little more pronounced with the passing of every season. And as her disease progressed, she needed more and more constant care and supervision. Celia didn't mind taking care of her mother. In fact, she enjoyed it. She just wished she had a home of her own to do it in.

It had been almost two years since her eldest sibling, Lucas, had shattered their beliefs of being a perfect family when he had revealed they had all been adopted. On the quest to learn the truth after their mother let it slip in a moment of haziness that she couldn't have children, Lucas had found love with Sarah.

Sarah was a wonderful sister-in-law and an even better daughter-in-law to their mother, but Celia could understand that after being married for eighteen months she had to be growing tired of having Lucas's siblings and his mother underfoot the whole time. Lucas, as the oldest son, inherited the family farm. And although he insisted he wanted to care for his sisters and his mother, Celia knew it was time for him to care for his own family.

After Daisy had run away to the city to find her birth parents, she had returned, grateful to be part of a loving family. Soon after, Ryan Ascot had had followed her home. With Lucas's permission, Ryan had joined the community and lived for six months in the hayloft before they had baptized him into the congregation.

Ryan had easily adapted to life in the Amish community and life on the farm and now had become Lucas's right-hand man. That was why when Ryan and Daisy had been married five months ago, Ryan had insisted that instead of finding a home of their own, they should build one on the farm.

Their cottage was on the other side of the farm, still keeping them close but giving everyone a little more privacy.

Everyone except for Celia.

She set the table, knowing that her family would join her for dinner soon since Ryan and Daisy still joined them most nights, and gathered her courage, knowing it was time for her to say her piece. As the middle-child Celia had always hated conflict and confrontation and she didn't plan on doing either tonight, but it was time her siblings understood how she felt.

Sarah would never dare suggest that Celia and her mother needed to move out, but Celia could understand it even without Sarah saying anything in that regard.

Newly married and with their first born on the way, Sarah and Lucas would need the room. More than anything, they needed the privacy and space to enjoy their new adventure as parents.

The wind rustled the tree in the backyard, sending orange leaves dancing on the breeze. For a moment, Celia stood there, mesmerized by its freedom. By its beauty.

"You're awfully quiet today," Sarah said behind her.

Celia turned to her sister-in-law with a smile in place. "Just lost in my own thoughts, I guess. I know that winter isn't much to look forward to, but I sure enjoy the fall. The beauty just amazes me every time."

Sarah agreed with a nod as she came to stand beside Celia. "Next fall I'll be a mamm."

Celia turned to Sarah with a loving smile. "And a wunderbaar mamm at that."

"I just checked on Lydia; she's sitting by the window without a care in the world. She asked for you?" Sarah mentioned as she poured them each a cup of tea.

"I'll go get her; everyone will be here for dinner soon." Celia made her way from the kitchen to the living room and for a moment just stood to one side, watching her mother. It broke her heart to know that her mother was slowly losing grasp of her memories and her mind. The disease had come on so suddenly the doctors had thought it was early onset aggressive Alzheimer's, but over the last year, its progression had slowed.

Celia thanked the Lord for that every day. She would cherish all the time she had left with her mother, but she cherished her mother's lucid moments even more. They were shorter now than they had been a year before, but at least there were times she still remembered.

"Mamm, would you like to join us in the kitchen for dinner?" Celia asked, kneeling in front of her mother.

"Dinner, but we just woke up. Isn't it breakfast?" Lydia asked, with a confused frown.

Celia smiled patiently. "You woke up from your afternoon nap. See, the sun is setting in the west," Celia pointed outside the window.

"Ach, of course. Where's my mind?" Lydia chuckled softly as she stood up. "I might have forgotten the time, but I can walk by myself, denke."

Celia followed her mother to the kitchen with a triumphant smile. Her mother might not always be lucid, but she was still as sharp as a tack with her sense of humor.

Just as they reached the kitchen, Daisy came through the backdoor. "Chicken fried steak? I swear you're Ryan's favorite schweschder-in-law."

Celia laughed. "I'm Ryan's only schweschder-in-law."

"You're my favorite as well," Sarah added with a smile as she offered Lydia a glass of milk.

"You might decide differently when you taste my potatoes. I think they're a little over salted," Celia admitted when the backdoor opened and Ryan and Lucas walked in.

"Salt has never been a problem for me." Ryan hung his hat behind the door. Lucas did the same.

"As a diner and not the cook, I refuse to pass out any criticism. Daed always said you don't criticize the cook unless you're planning on cooking the next meal and doing it better." Lucas took his seat at the head of the table.

Celia nodded with a smile at the memory. Daisy was very young when they'd lost their father, but Lucas had many fond memories of him since they had worked together in the fields.

For a few moments, the kitchen erupted in organized chaos. Food was plated, cold drinks were poured, tea was made, and all the while Celia felt her mother watching them from her place at the table.

She realized that her mother became a little withdrawn when there were too many people around. Celia took a seat beside her mother, their plates laden with chicken fried steak, mashed potatoes, and soft-cooked sweet peas.

"Let us bow our heads in silent prayer," Lucas's voice was deep before he was the first to bow his head.

Once everyone had said their silent prayers of thanks, Celia glanced around the table. She loved having her whole family around her. That's what made what she had to say even harder.

She didn't want her siblings to think that she didn't love them, only that they were all outgrowing their roles in the family. It was time for new roles to be assigned, and tonight Celia was going to be the one to broach the subject.

She took a bite of her chicken fried steak and hoped it would give her the courage she needed.

Chapter 2
Everything Changes

"So it seems that your boppli won't have to wait too long before it will have a cousin."

Everyone at the table turned to look at Daisy with surprise.

Sarah had just returned from putting their mother to bed, while Celia and Daisy had cleaned the kitchen. They all sat with coffee, enjoying the wind down of another family dinner, when Daisy made the announcement.

Although she was still nervous about what she wanted to talk to her siblings about, Celia felt her mouth curve and her heart swell with joy. There were tears of joy welling in her younger sister's eyes. "Daisy, that's wunderbaar news. Congratulations!"

"Congratulations! How far along are you?" Sarah asked, her hand instinctively resting on her slightly swollen belly.

Daisy smiled even broader when Ryan laid a hand on her shoulder. "Only two months, I went to the Englisch doctor today. I thought the tiredness and nausea was a flu."

"That's truly wunderbar," Sarah gushed. "That means our bopplis will only be four months apart."

"Jah." Daisy nodded.

"Congratulations, Daisy." Lucas smiled at Daisy with brotherly affection. "Cottage might get too small sooner than we thought."

Celia enjoyed her coffee as she listened to Daisy and Sarah exchanging information about their pregnancies, while the men talked about the farm, as they usually did.

She waited until there was a lull in the conversation when she cleared her throat. "Actually, there was something I was meaning to talk to you about, if you're not in too much of a hurry Daisy?"

Daisy shook her head. "Not at all."

"Why didn't you tell us over dinner, then Mamm would've heard as well?" Lucas interrupted.

Daisy shrugged. "When I tell Mamm, I want her to be lucid. I want it to be just the two of us, and I want it to be special."

"So we're not special," Lucas teased playfully.

"Celia, you were saying?" Sarah asked, gently directing the attention back to Celia.

Celia nodded. "Jah. I've been thinking it's time for Mamm and I to get a place of our own." She held up her hand when both her siblings opened their mouths. "Let me finish first, please."

When they nodded, Celia drew in a fortifying breath before she continued.

"Lucas, you and Sarah are expecting your first boppli in less than three months. I know you don't mind having Mamm and I here, but don't you think your frau would appreciate being the frau of her own household when she becomes a mamm? Sarah, I know you've never complained about having us here, but keep in mind, this house is only so big. With Mamm growing older, we all know her care is going to become more and more demanding. You're going to have a boppli and hopefully more to follow soon after that will demand your attention."

"We help with Mamm," Lucas said defensively.

"I never said you didn't," Celia said firmly. "You know I don't mind taking care of Mamm. I'm not saying this as a martyr, I'm saying this as a grown woman that needs to find her own life instead of impeding on her siblings' families."

"This is preposterous," Daisy said, shaking her head with a crease between her brows. "If the house is too small, Lucas can add to it. You and Mamm aren't going anywhere."

Celia had known it would come to an argument, but she wouldn't back down from her position.

She turned to Sarah and Lucas. "You need a room for the nursery. That means Mamm and I will have to share a room when the boppli comes."

"If taking care of Mamm is getting the better of you, we can take turns. She can stay here one week and with me and Ryan the next," Daisy suggested.

Celia frowned at her sister with a baffled look. "You want to shuffle Mamm back and forth? She's already confused most days. How much more confusing would that be?"

"Until a year ago, we all lived together with no problems. I just don't see what the problem is now?" Lucas sounded almost agitated with Celia.

"Because a year ago, Ryan wasn't here. Because a year ago you weren't expecting a boppli, neither was Daisy. And because a year ago, the situation suited all of us. When Ryan and Daisy got married, you didn't hesitate to help them build a home of their own. So just because I'm not married, I don't get to have a say in what I want?" Celia asked stubbornly.

Lucas's eyes widened with surprise at her brash tone. "Celia, of course, we care about what you want."

"Really? Because no one has asked me. Ever," Celia snapped back. "When Daed passed, and you took over the farm, I took over helping Mamm with the haus and caring for Daisy. When Mamm got sick, I took over the housekeeping and cared for her. When Daisy wanted to become teacher's assistant, I didn't hesitate to give her the opportunity. I've never hesitated in helping either of you. I've cared for this haus," Celia's eyes scanned the room, "for you, and for Mamm my whole life. I wouldn't want to live my life any other way. I cherish each moment I can cook for you, or sit with Mamm, or fold your laundry, but I need to have a little space of my own. Just like you deserve to have privacy with your family, I need to have it now and then. I know this is the right thing to do, so why are you so against it?"

Celia didn't wait for them to respond, instead she stood up and left the kitchen. She closed her bedroom door behind her and waited for her racing heart to slow down. She had never walked out on a conversation before, but she'd realized that if she didn't leave, she might say things she might regret later.

A tear slipped over her cheek as she sat down on the bed. If her siblings wouldn't understand, then there was only one person who would.

Gott.

She prayed for guidance, patience, and, most of all, for the understanding of her siblings. By the time she curled up in bed, she hoped Gott would bless her with a miracle.

The miracle of her own home where she could care for her mother without worrying about waking the baby, or intruding on Sarah and Lucas's privacy.

Chapter 3
The Invisible Pillar

After what happened after dinner, it wasn't surprising to Lucas that he couldn't sleep. He rolled from side to side while Sarah restfully slept beside him. His mind kept turning over and over about what Celia had said.

Had none of them truly ever asked her what she wanted?

He couldn't help but feel overwhelmed with guilt. He had been so busy focusing on the farm and taking over from his father, that he hadn't once stopped for a moment to think that Celia might have dreams of her own.

His heart skipped a beat at the thought of Celia leaving. For the first time, Lucas realized he depended on Celia for almost everything in his life. Although he and Sarah were married, it was still Celia who cooked most of their meals. It was Celia who did their laundry, who cleaned their house, who cared for his mother... And so the list went on and on.

Of course, Sarah had taken over some of the household chores, but with her working in town for three days a week, Celia usually did Sarah's chores as well. Without Celia, Lucas wasn't sure how he or Daisy would've managed until now.

Especially with their mother.

When their mother became delusional, Celia was patient and gentle and never got angry or upset. Celia knew how to calm her down when she was angry over something that happened years ago, or how to console her when she cried about losing her husband for the hundredth time. The pillar of their family was Celia.

Something Lucas had always thought he was, until tonight.

He shoved back the covers and tossed his legs over the side of the bed. The evenings were growing cooler every night, he realized. Guilt washed over him again, realizing he had never had to ask for extra blankets on his bed. It was as if Celia knew precisely what time of year to add more blankets or to remove them.

Lucas shook his head and walked to the kitchen, hoping that a glass of water would flush away the guilt. He'd never seen Celia so upset before, and he couldn't help but feel responsible for it. He poured himself a glass of water and took a seat at the kitchen table with nothing but the moonlight shining in from the window for light.

"Lucas! You scared me!" Celia's voice was barely more than a whisper from the doorway. "I didn't think anyone was awake."

Although she had been upset earlier, there was no sign of her harboring any anger towards Lucas now. "I couldn't sleep. You neither?"

"Nee, sleep wouldn't come," Celia admitted, grabbing an apple from the fruit basket. She took a seat at the table and met Lucas's gaze. "I'm sorry about earlier. I know it was rude of me to just leave like that. I'll apologize to Sarah, Ryan, and Daisy tomorrow."

Lucas shook his head. "You have nothing to apologize for. Nothing, you hear me? Everything you said was true. I just don't think Daisy, or I were prepared to hear it."

"I didn't mean to upset you," Celia sighed.

"Perhaps it was necessary because I think I finally understand. You don't want to live here anymore. Did you get a job in town?" Lucas asked, wondering if that might be the reason for her sudden change of heart.

Celia smiled sadly. "Lucas, why would I do that? I love my life. I love the chores, I love taking care of Mamm, I love going to my quilting group... Unless you and Sarah can't afford to care for me and Mamm anymore with the boppli coming?"

"Mamm is my responsibility and as for you, I feel guilty for not paying you a wage for all you've done for us over the years. Do you have a place in mind for you and Mamm?" Lucas asked.

"Nee. But I'm sure we'll be able to find something close enough so we can visit often. We need little. Just two bedrooms, perhaps a third one for when I'm taking care of my nieces and nephews." Celia added with a wink. "Perhaps I can arrange for a reduced rental fee if I do the yardwork and things like that... It's just something I'm thinking about, Lucas."

"Well, stop thinking about it." Lucas said, reaching for her hand, knowing he was doing the right thing. "I'll build you a haus."

"What?" Celia's eyes widened with surprise. "Lucas, that isn't necessary."

"Of course it is. You're right, you deserve some privacy and Sarah deserves to be the frau of her own household. And if I build it, it can be close enough to walk over to see you and Mamm every day. If you need to go somewhere, Sarah or I can watch Mamm, and you'll have a place to call your own."

"You'd really do that?" Celia asked, looking at him with admiration in her eyes. Lucas couldn't remember the last time Celia had looked at him like that.

"Definitely. We can start tomorrow by picking out the right spot. You better start thinking of what you want it to be like. Would you like your kitchen or your bedroom facing east, then you can watch the sunset on the porch?" Lucas suggested.

Celia's face lit up like a child's at the sight of a wrapped gift. "I can have a porch?"

"Don't you worry about the cost, Celia. I'll take care of it. You just worry about what you want. I'm never not taking your dreams into account ever again."

"Lucas, you barely have time for the farm now that you and Ryan have planted more crops this year. How will you ever have time to build a house before the boppli comes?"

Lucas smiled at her with promise in his eyes. "Daed made provisions for expansions Celia. We'll hire someone to do it. The best carpenter in the community if he's available. Daniel Stoltzfus?"

"Ach Lucas, this is the best news ever. I really hope he's available. I dreaded the idea of moving away from the farm, but I knew it would've been for the best. You and Sarah deserve a home of your own." Celia smiled gratefully.

"Gut, now that's settled. You think we might try for a little sleep?" Lucas asked, standing up.

A large yawn escaped Celia. "Definitely."

They shared a smile before they each headed to their bedrooms. This time, when Lucas climbed into bed, he felt peace wash over him instead of guilt. He might not have understood Celia's motivations or reasons, but to see the joy in her eyes when he told her he'd build her a house on the property—he no longer cared about the reason.

He just cared to give Celia what she truly wanted.

A home of her own.

Chapter 4
A Perfect Spot

Daniel Stoltzfus was pleased to get a message from Lucas Eymann about quoting on a new home on the property. As a fifth-generation carpenter, Daniel not only took pride in his work but he thoroughly enjoyed it.

He enjoyed it even more when he was working with someone in the community. Since there wasn't always work in the community, he often took jobs from Englischers in town as well. But Lucas's request had come at exactly the right time. Daniel had just finished his latest project in town and was about to put out feelers about new projects.

As he drove the buggy to the Eymann farm, Daniel realized that he and Lucas had known each other since before they had attended the one-room schoolhouse together as first graders. Although the old memory was hazy, he could still remember a barn raising at the height of summer where he and Lucas had pretended to be building a barn of their own with the scraps of wood that lay piled as high as they were.

He had attended Lucas's wedding a little over a year ago and Daisy's wedding six months ago. Daniel was happy that the Eymann family were finding happiness after all the troubles they had faced over the last few years.

Daniel respected Lucas for taking over the farm when his father passed away. Although he had only been sixteen, Lucas had quickly picked up the slack and took the reins. When word of Lydia Eymann's Alzheimer's had reached Daniel, he had felt sympathy for the siblings that would now have to care for their mother.

But the Eymann family had always stood together, just like they did now with the care of their ailing mother.

The Eymann farm came into sight; it was on the other side of the community from where Daniel lived. It surprised him to see how tall the crops were and how many there were. Harvest was only a few weeks away and Daniel could already tell it was going to be a record year for Lucas and his family.

Today it didn't feel as if Daniel was going to see a client to quote on a new project, instead as he drove through the gates of the Eymann farm, it felt as if he was going to visit an old friend. The barn stood proudly with its red and white trim on one side, with the main homestead to the right. Between the two, there was a kitchen garden, a chicken coop, and the water pump. The yard was neat and didn't have a single thing out of place. Even the buggy seemed to have its designated spot.

Daniel let out a sigh as he brought his buggy to a stop. If only his workshop could look as neat as the Eymann's farm. But being passionate about his work often left Daniel distracted and hastily following an idea, without paying much attention to returning tools to their storage or cleaning as he worked.

The chaotic workshop worked perfectly for Daniel. Although to anyone else it would look as if a hurricane had blown through, Daniel knew where every item was, no matter how big or how small.

He climbed out of the buggy and glanced around for Lucas, but Lucas was nowhere in sight. After checking the time on his pocket watch, Daniel wondered if Lucas had forgotten their meeting.

The backdoor opened and Celia, Lucas's sister, rushed out.

"Daniel, I'm so sorry. I completely forgot about our meeting. I began washing the windows and only remembered when I saw your buggy. Please forgive how disheveled I look," Celia quickly apologized with an apologetic smile.

For a moment, Daniel was at a loss for words. He saw Celia from a distance at Sunday Services, but he couldn't remember the last time he'd actually had a conversation with her. Two years, perhaps four years ago. She remained home to care for their mother most of the time, which made talking to her even more of a challenge.

But now that he stood in front of her, so close that he could touch her if he took a step forward, Daniel couldn't help but notice how beautiful Celia had become. The little girl with fair white hair and green eyes the color of fresh leaves had turned into a magnificent woman. She was tall, lithe, and her smile did something to Daniel he couldn't quite understand.

"If you'd rather come back another time, I'd understand," Celia offered another apology.

Daniel blinked to gather his thoughts. "Nee, nee, it's perfectly fine. I just thought I'd be meeting with Lucas, that's all."

"Sorry to disappoint you, but the home we need building is for me and my mamm. Since Lucas is busy getting ready for harvest, I'll be the one running point on this project," Celia explained.

Daniel usually hated working with women. They always changed their minds at the last minute, never really knew what they wanted and fussed over inconsequential things like the color of nails. But with Celia, somehow, he couldn't wait to get started.

"A haus you say? That's exciting. Where do you have in mind?" Daniel asked, glancing around the yard.

Celia's smile broadened as she pointed to an old oak tree a few hundred yards from the house. "There. I'd like to sit in the shade on scorching afternoons and watch it turn as the season changes. That way Lucas can still keep an eye on us, but we're far enough to each enjoy our own space."

Daniel smiled, feeling more excited about this project than he'd been about any other project in the past. "That sure is the perfect spot to build a haus. Why don't we walk over and you tell me what you have in mind?"

Chapter 5
A Curious Meeting

Celia stopped beneath the old oak tree and turned to Daniel with a hopeful smile. "So, how soon can you start?"

She tried to ignore the skip of her heart when Daniel chuckled. He had become quite handsome since the time he attended school with Lucas. Daniel was tall with broad shoulders. His face looked chiseled with a square jaw, but his eyes were kind. Right now he was smiling at her with a twinkle in his eyes. Was he mocking her?

"Right now," Daniel said with his smile still in place. "The first step is to tell me what you have in mind. Then I draw up a plan and if you're happy with it, I can put in an order for the lumber. But first, I need to know what you need?"

Celia felt the corners of her mouth curve. "Then let's begin. Mamm and I don't need much. I was thinking two bedrooms would be more than enough. Perhaps a kitchen that opens up into the living room. That way I can keep an eye on her when I'm cooking. The bathroom needs to have a shower and a bath..."

Celia trailed off and caught her mind running in a different direction.

"You were saying?" Daniel encouraged her.

Celia quickly brushed away a tear that had escaped her eyes. "It's hard to say this out loud, but I need to think of the future. Mamm's disease might affect her mobility later…"

Ever since her mother had been diagnosed, Celia had tried her best not to think of what could happen. She avoided thinking about the final stages of Alzheimer's and, most of all, she refused to even talk about it.

But now, as she stood on the grass where she wanted to make a home for her and her mother, Celia realized that although her mother was perfectly mobile at the moment, that could change in the future. Lucas's home wasn't built to host a wheelchair, but Celia's new home had to be wheelchair friendly.

She turned to Daniel and saw kindness and empathy in his gaze.

"I understand. You need the house to be wheelchair-friendly," Daniel nodded. "I can make the doorways and passages a little wider, make sure there are no variations in the levels of the house and the shower can be a walk in, so if that happens, you can wheel her into the bathroom and help her into a shower chair?"

Daniel had thought of more ways to accommodate a wheelchair than Celia ever would've. "That sounds gut."

"For now, the home will just seem a little more spacious, so no one would even know we've planned ahead. I'll still build steps to the front and back doors as well. When the time comes, which I'll pray never happens, I can easily convert the steps into ramps," Daniel explained.

Celia brushed away another tear, this time a tear of gratitude. "Denke Daniel. I'd appreciate it if you didn't mention this to Lucas or Daisy. I don't want them to be reminded of what might still happen."

"Of course not. Besides, it's your project, your home," Daniel confirmed before he walked over and looked out over the crop fields. "This view is simply breathtaking. You should have a window facing this way. Perhaps from the living room?"

Celia smiled. "Jah, I'll put a chair there for Mamm. She enjoys sitting by the window."

"Right, for the kitchen. Do you have anything specific in mind?" Daniel asked, glancing around the area.

"I haven't really thought of the kitchen. I guess a kitchen is a kitchen, a pantry would be a bonus, of course. There is one thing I thought of. I'd like the washing line to be out of sight from Lucas's home. Their washing line is on the other side, so I wouldn't want them staring into our laundry on wash day."

Daniel chuckled. "I see you've thought of the most important things."

Excitement built in Celia as her dream home appeared in her mind's eye. "A porch! I'd love a porch."

"I'll add that to the list. Anything else? Perhaps a small mudroom off the kitchen. I've found that most parents have them added on later, to avoid the muddy mess of young children rushing indoors." Daniel suggested.

Celia's heart stopped for a moment. She had only been thinking of her and her mother with planning her new home. Not for once had she thought that it might be the home where she would one day raise a family. She was only twenty-four, but compared to the other women of her age in the community, she was probably already called a spinster.

Not that Celia didn't think of finding love and having a family, it was simply a matter of never having the time or inclination to find someone worthy of her heart. She firmly believed that when Gott thought the time was right, he would send the right man to her.

"I… Isn't that planning a little too far in the future?" Celia asked, shaking her head with a doubtful look.

"What might seem extravagant to you now will provide a little more comfort in the future. It's easier to add a few square feet when we build from scratch than to add it on later and struggle with leaks and other problems. If you're worried about the cost, it won't make a significant difference at all." Daniel searched her eyes as if he saw something there he was curious about.

It made Celia's cheeks heat with a light blush. "Then I guess it's all right." Feeling a little flustered, she smiled at him with a curious look. "Don't you need to be writing all of this down?"

Daniel shook his head. "I have a terrible memory, especially with things like crops, gardening, and the weather. But with carpentry, my mind is like a sponge. I think I have everything I need to draw up a plan. I can have it for you within a couple of days. Can I stop by Friday?"

Friday was only two days away, Celia thought, as they walked back to Daniel's buggy. It seemed he was in just as a hurry as she was to get the ball rolling on her home. "Friday is fine. Perhaps late afternoon, if you don't mind. I'd like Lucas to look at them as well."

"Then I'll plan my day accordingly," Daniel said as he stopped beside his buggy. He searched her gaze for a moment before he smiled. "I look forward to building you your new home, Celia. I hope I can make it everything you'd like it to be."

Celia's heart fluttered again. "I'm sure you will. Denke for coming, Daniel."

As Daniel rode away, Celia watched. She remembered Daniel from when they were young, but back then, he didn't make her heart flutter or look at her with curiosity.

Just like she couldn't remember looking at him with that same curiosity.

Chapter 6
Let Faith Be Your Guide

It wasn't every day Daniel was contracted to build a new home. A project of that caliber usually excited him, but as he sat down at the dining room to draw, he found himself more excited than usual.

He reached for the plans he had drawn up for homes in the past and went over each one with Celia in mind. With building a home, especially an Amish home, there weren't usually many luxuries or even decorative facets to keep in mind. Just like the name suggested, Amish people liked plain homes.

Houses with few but large rooms. A big kitchen and a nice porch were usually the only prerequisites. But as he inspected the plans he had drawn up for houses in the past, Daniel found not one of them suitable. He used certain designs as a baseline for new projects, but it only took him a few moments to realize that with Celia's home, only something fresh and tailored to her and her mother's needs would do.

With a pocketknife, he sharpened his pencil when he heard his father's footsteps behind him. "New project?"

As Daniel had not yet married, he didn't see a reason to leave his childhood home just yet. His parents were both alive and healthy, and he enjoyed their company.

"Jah. A haus for the Eymann family. Lucas and his wife are keeping the main haus and Celia and her mamm want something close by. Something of their own," Daniel explained as he drew the outlines of the yard and marking a 'X' where the large tree stood.

"That sounds promising. You enjoy doing something from scratch," his father said, taking a seat beside him. "You have a design in mind?"

"Nee," Daniel said, shaking his head. "I want it to be functional, but I want it to be unique as well. Celia has all but devoted her life to caring for her mamm and now, with her siblings married, she's taking over the care of their mamm altogether."

"Admirable girl, I'd say," his father said, standing up. "I'm going to keep your mamm company in the kitchen, but I'd like to see what you've done when you're finished."

Daniel chuckled. "To be finished, I need to have an idea first."

"You've always built from the heart and with faith, start there and the ideas will come," his father encouraged him with a smile before leaving him.

Daniel smiled and shook his head at his father's advice. If someone had to ask, Daniel wouldn't hesitate to say he had the best parents in the world. They were supportive, kind, and loving, and would turn to their faith if they didn't have the answers.

They were wonderful mentors and even better parents. Daniel considered them friends.

He closed his eyes, asked the Lord to guide the pencil in his hand, to guide his thoughts and to open his mind to creativity. When he opened his eyes, a quiet peace settled over him. It calmed his excitement just enough to focus.

With smooth, carefully focused movements, he drew. When he had an idea, he would lean back in his chair and glance around their own home to consider the functionality and cost before he would incorporate it into the design.

Twice, he crumpled up his design sheets, only to begin again.

When he built a home for Celia and her mamm, he wanted it to be perfect.

"Dinner is on the table," his father called from the kitchen.

Daniel went to join his parents and eagerly told them about his project.

His father was just as excited as he was, making it clear he didn't doubt Daniel's abilities for a moment. But his mother seemed a little demurer.

"I'm happy for you Daniel, truly I am. But don't you think it's time you focused a little more on building your own life?" his mother asked with a gentle frown.

Daniel felt taken aback for a moment. "You want me to move out, Mamm?"

"Nee! Of course not. Your daed and I love having you around. I just think... Daniel, you haven't attended a singing in over two years. I can't remember the last time you took a girl on a buggy ride. You're not getting any younger, you know," his mother reminded him.

Daniel let out a sigh. His parents rarely tried to interfere in his life, but his mother had brought up her concerns about his married status a few times in the past. "Mamm, look at you and Daed. Did Daed go to singings for years on end to find the right frau?"

His mother blushed and laughed. "Nee, he found her by the side of the road with a broken buggy wheel and a stubborn horse. Gut thing he was a carpenter, or I might still have been sitting there."

Daniel chuckled. His father was also a carpenter but focused more on furniture, whereas Daniel focused more on construction. "Exactly. Gott had a plan for you to meet and when the time was right, he made it so. I believe Gott has a plan for me as well and when the time is right, I'll meet the right frau. But until then I will not sit around and wait for her or give other women false hope by taking them on buggy rides I don't intend to repeat."

"Spoken like a wise man," his father agreed.

"Ach… it's just I'm not getting younger. I'd like to play with my grandchildren while I can still chase after them and play with them."

Daniel laughed. "Mamm, you're not old just yet. There is still time."

"So, have you come up with an idea yet?"

Daniel nodded at his father. "I'm going to make it an open plan home. Almost like the homes the Englischers like so much. Where the kitchen, the dining room and the living room all flows into each other. I know it's not really custom with Amish homes but it will be much more practical for Celia and her mamm."

Daniel didn't add that it would make life easier when Lydia was confined to a wheelchair if such a day would ever come.

"I like the idea. I've been in homes like that before. It feels so spacious and it's much easier to keep tidy since you only have one space to clear," his mother added, pleased.

Daniel smiled. "That's what I was thinking. One bedroom with a bathroom on one side and on the other two more bedrooms with a small bathroom."

"That's a gut idea, considering each will have a little privacy."

The conversation continued to circle around ideas for the design of the house and which windows should look out over which area. By the time dinner was over, Daniel already knew he wouldn't be able to sleep tonight. He had too many ideas he wanted to incorporate into his design before he forgot.

After his parents retired for the night, Daniel put a fresh pot of coffee on the wood stove and moved his work to the kitchen table.

He sat there designing Celia's home while thinking of her the entire time. By the time he was finished, the sun was already poking its head over the horizon.

Chapter 7
Designing a Dream

On Friday afternoon, Celia sat with her mother by the window in the living room, anxiously waiting for Daniel to arrive.

She couldn't wait to see the plans or learn about the ideas he had for her new home. Over the last two days she had even played with the idea of her own kitchen garden. Just as quickly as the idea had formed in her mind, she had shoved it aside.

One kitchen garden between two homes was more than enough.

Instead, she would focus on a few flower beds and perhaps to sell more of her quilting to save for a rocking chair for the porch. She could already imagine herself quilting on the porch, with her mother sitting by her side enjoying the fresh air.

"Is he here yet?" Lucas asked, coming in through the kitchen.

"Nee. I asked him to come late afternoon. We didn't set a specific time," Celia explained as she stood up.

She glanced at the clock on the wall and noticed it was already almost five o'clock. "I better get started on dinner. Will you sit with Mamm?"

Lucas smiled as he took a seat across from his mother. "How was your day, Mamm?"

She turned to Lucas with a hazy smile. Today was one of her worse days. Her mother had been confused for most of the day. Celia watched from the door, her heart breaking when she remembered that this was how Lucas had learned about their adoptions. Her mother had a moment of lucidity that Lucas had confused for a delusion when she had told him she couldn't have children.

The news had bothered Lucas at first. As for Daisy, it had been earth shattering. Daisy had found her birth mother only a year before. It had taken her all the way to Millersburg only to learn that her birth mother didn't want any contact with her at all.

The only good thing to come of the experience was her marriage to Ryan.

At the time he had been Englisch, only to convert after falling in love with both Daisy and her Amish faith.

"Hullo. Are you the new bishop?" Lydia asked, turning to Lucas.

Lucas smiled. Most of the time, they had stopped trying to correct her when she got things wrong. "Jah, would you like me to pray with you?"

Lydia sighed gratefully. "Denke, bishop. I've been feeling strange of late, perhaps a prayer for my health?"

Lucas reached for his mother's hands and prayed.

Celia moved to the kitchen to give them some privacy. She swallowed past the lump in her throat, struggling to accept her mother's condition. When her siblings had learned they were adopted, it had bothered them.

Only Celia hadn't felt that way.

For her it had been easy to forgive the lies of omission, because in her mind she only ever had the Eymann's for parents. Lydia might not remember her every day, but Lydia had been there for her every step of her childhood. Just like her father, Noah, had been a kind but firm father.

Celia didn't need to learn more about her life before she was adopted. She had peace knowing that this was where Gott had wanted her to be, and that this was where she wanted to be.

She peeled some potatoes and put them on to boil before sliding a ham into the oven.Celia had taken it out of the icebox earlier that day for that purpose. The carrots and peas followed next. By the time Sarah arrived home from working in town for the day, dinner just needed to be supervised.

Daisy and Ryan weren't coming over tonight, so when Daniel came, it would be Sarah that needed to keep an eye on the food while she and Lucas met with him.

"He's here," Lucas called from the living room.

Celia quickly untied her cooking apron before she turned to Sarah. "Will you sit with Mamm? The food ought to be fine on its own. You might just keep an eye on the carrots."

"Of course. Good luck," Sarah wished her before she moved to the living room to sit with Lydia.

Celia and Lucas met Daniel on the porch. After the men shook hands and asked after each other's health, Daniel turned to Celia with a broad smile. "I either got it right, or I got it terribly wrong."

Celia laughed nervously. "I'm sure you got it right."

"Let's see," Daniel said, following Lucas inside.

Daniel opened the sketches on the living room table before he turned to Lucas. Celia listened absentmindedly as he explained about measurements of the house, the rooms and the yard.

She studied the sketches, understanding most of it, but wondering where the walls were. When Daniel finally turned to her, her heart skipped a beat.

"Right, I know this isn't your usual Amish home, but I thought you might like something a little more functional," Daniel explained. "Usually Amish homes in our community have separate kitchens, living rooms, and dining rooms. In this instance, I did away with walls entirely in the living area."

Celia frowned before it made sense. "So this entire space will be open?"

"That's right," Daniel nodded. "So this large open space in the center will be your living area. You'll have the kitchen on the left in the back, with the living room next to it. The dining area is here next to the porch. So when you open your front door, you will walk into a small open space with the dining room to your left."

"That's... different..." Lucas commented, sounding a little baffled.

"That way, when your mamm is sitting by the window overlooking the fields, you can have an eye on her from everywhere in this area." Daniel explained.

"That's wunderbar, Daniel," Celia smiled gratefully. Clearly, he had listened when she had explained about what they needed.

"Between the kitchen and the dining room, you will have a door leading to a passage on the left. There is a large bedroom and a full-size bathroom. Then over there," Daniel pointed to the other side of the house. "You will have a door leading to another passageway between the living room and the dining room. Here you have two bedrooms with a smaller bathroom that both rooms can access."

"That's... You thought ahead..." Celia chuckled. "This side is for Mamm, and this side is for when I have kinner?"

Daniel shrugged with a knowing look. "I told you it's better to plan long term."

Lucas pointed to a small room that led off the kitchen behind Lydia's room. "What's that?"

"That's the mud room. It will have morning light, so you don't need to fuss with lanterns in winter after doing the chores, and it can double as a laundry room as well," Daniel explained. "It leads into the kitchen, the heart of the home."

"So Mamm's window will face north towards Lucas's home and my window will face east?" Celia asked, trying to adjust her mind to the directions.

"Jah, I thought you might like to rise with the sun and watch the sunsets on the porch. From there, you can see your nieces and nephews play in Lucas's yard as well."

Lucas chuckled. "Daniel, I knew they said you thought of everything, but this... you truly did think of everything. I just have a question about heat. The rooms seem far apart—how do you propose to keep them heated in winter?"

Daniel pointed to the design. "The woodstove in the kitchen will be against the wall that hosts your mother's bedroom on the other side. As the woodstove is burning throughout winter, that room will be comfortably heated. As for the summer, if she opens the windows, the breeze will blow out the heat when you open the front door." Daniel turned to Celia. "The fireplace in the living room is next to your room, which means just like your mother's rooms, it will be warm throughout winter."

"Wunderbaar," Celia said, clapping her hands together. "This is really beautiful. But…" Celia turned to Lucas. "Isn't it big for just me and Mamm? I mean, it's lovely, but why go through all that expense for just two people? It's bigger than the home you built for Daisy and Ryan?"

Lucas shook his head. "Daisy and Ryan can easily add to their home when the time comes. But I agree with Daniel. This design, this layout, is perfect. This way, you can care for Mamm and still have some privacy of your own. When the time comes… after… you and your mann can move into Mamm's room and the kinner can have the rooms on the other side of the haus."

Celia swallowed past the lump in her throat. She didn't want to think that far ahead, but Lucas was right. It made perfect sense. And that Daniel had designed the entire house to be wheelchair friendly without Lucas even noticing made it so much better. This will be her forever home, Celia decided right there and then.

"Denke, Lucas. I love it. If you're sure, I'm happy to move ahead."

"You heard my schweschder. When can you start?" Lucas asked, turning to Daniel.

Daniel laughed and handed Lucas a document. "There's the estimated cost of the project as well as how much deposit I would need to order the first purchase of lumber."

Lucas frowned and Celia felt her hopes crash into the dirt. It was too expensive.

"Daniel, I think there's a mistake on this. It can't be right?" Lucas turned to Daniel.

Daniel shook his head. "I'm sorry Lucas, but the cost of lumber has increased exponentially over the last few months. I can cut down on the cost of labor if it's too much, or we can work out something else?"

Lucas's eyes widened with shock. "You think this is too much? It's too little. This is about what it cost me to build Daisy's home. If I'd known you could do it for this price, I would've never even considered building it myself. I'll go to the bank tomorrow. In the meantime, could you perhaps give me an estimate of what it would cost to add another two bedrooms to Daisy's cottage?"

"Of course, although I'd prefer to finish this project first," Daniel agreed.

"Gut, then, everyone is happy. Daisy and Ryan get a bigger cottage, you and Mamm have a dream home of your own, and Sarah and I have space for when her cousin from Ohio comes to visit after the boppli is born," Lucas sounded pleased as he and Daniel shook hands.

Celia wanted to jump up and down with joy, but she held herself back and simply smiled. "Denke Lucas... and Daniel."

Daniel turned to her with a broad smile. "Don't thank me just yet. Let's get it built first."

Chapter 8
Another Bad Day

Celia waited for Lucas to come in for tea on Monday morning. Since Sarah was at work in town and Daisy was at school, he was the only sibling available to talk to. She put on a fresh pot of coffee, checking in on her mother every few minutes.

The anxiety that had built in her since the morning seemed to have reached a boiling point. She needed to get her mother to the doctor and without Lucas or someone to help her, it was simply impossible unless she called for an Englisch driver.

Something she wouldn't do without Lucas's approval. Considering the cost, she always consulted with him first.

"It's chilly this morning," Lucas said, coming in through the back door with Ryan following on his heels. "We decided we deserved a cup of hot kaffe before returning to the fields."

Celia smiled, but it didn't reach her eyes. "Lucas, I need to talk to you about Mamm."

Lucas frowned. "Did something happen?" he asked even as he walked to the living room. "Where is she?"

"She's sleeping… again…" Celia explained as she handed them each a cup of coffee. "On Saturday, she was more tired than usual. I thought she was coming down with the flu or something. Yesterday she slept for most of the day, and this morning..." Celia's voice cracked with emotion.

Lucas set down his cup and moved towards her. "Celia, talk to me."

Celia shook her head. "She had trouble walking on her own, Lucas. I had to help her to the bathroom. I had to help her dress... something is wrong, Lucas."

Lucas nodded. "Anything else you're concerned about? Is she having an episode, perhaps?"

"Nee, she's not confused or angry. In fact, she's hardly talking at all. I don't know what's going on, but I know that something has changed. I really think we need to get her to the specialist. Perhaps it's her disease, but what if it's something else and we ignore it because we think it's just her disease?"

"Jah, you're right, we need to get her to the doctor. Would you like me to take you? Ryan can stay on here on the farm." Lucas offered kindly.

Celia nodded. "Jah, perhaps the buggy ride will do her gut as well. You know how she hates Englisch cars."

Lucas set down his mug. "I'll go hitch the buggy. You try to wake her up."

Celia nodded. "Denke Lucas."

"Nee," Lucas said, stepping forward and touching Celia's shoulder before meeting her gaze. "Denke for taking such gut care of her. I didn't even think anything of it when she slept for most of the day yesterday. It's because you're so observant that we caught her disease early. You're a Gott sent, schweschder."

Celia smiled, although her heart was crying. She didn't want to go to the doctor. She feared they would receive more devastating news. But she knew it was the right thing to do.

"I'll go get Mamm," Celia said, focusing on the problem instead of her emotions.

"I'll go help you with the horse and the buggy," Ryan offered, following Lucas out of the house.

Celia knew how it went. Sometimes it would only be a doctor's visit, other times her mother would be admitted for a few days for tests. For that reason, she packed an overnight bag with a set of clean clothes, two sets of night dresses, and her mother's toiletries. When the bag was packed and waiting by the front door, she moved to her mother's bedroom.

Lydia lay in bed, fast asleep, as if it was the middle of the night.

"Mamm," Celia spoke softly as she took a seat beside her mother on the bed. "Mamm, it's time to wake up."

Lydia sighed heavily in her sleep before her eyes fluttered open. "Do you know where the girls are? Are they at school?"

Celia nodded, realizing her mother was having a delusion. "Jah, they're at school. Noah took them."

"Bless his heart. What's wrong dear, goodness I only realize now I'm still in bed," Lydia said, glancing down at the bed in surprise.

"You're not feeling too well, so Noah asked me to take you to the Englisch doctor." Celia hated telling these fibs, but it was easier than upsetting her mother by trying to remind her of the present.

"Ach, Noah is overly cautious. I'm sure it's just the flu," Lydia argued with a smile.

"Either way, he wants to be sure. Kumm, let me help you up," Celia offered, standing up from the bed.

Lydia laughed as she turned to throw her legs over the side of the bed. "I told you, I'm fine."

Just as she tried to stand up, Celia noticed her one leg giving way. Celia stepped forward and caught her mother beneath the arms just in time to stop her from falling. "Here, let me help you."

Lydia leaned on her with frightened eyes filled with despair. "What's wrong with me? Who are you? Where are we?"

These moments of confusion were also more prevalent than a few months ago, Celia realized. "I'm Celia. You're at home and you're not feeling well. If you kumm with me, the Englisch doctor can help."

"All right, jah, I'll go. But I need to be home before the girls get out of school. Daisy doesn't do her homework if I'm not here and Celia will take to cooking without supervision," Lydia explained like a concerned mother of two young girls. She didn't realize that Celia was helping her towards the front door and hadn't been to school in years.

Curious about the timeline of her mother's illusion, Celia asked about her daughters. "How old are they?"

"Celia is twelve. She's a real little mother, always caring for Daisy and looking out for her bruder. Then there's Daisy, bright as a flower and stubborn as a thorn. She keeps all of us on our toes."

"They sound wunderbar," Celia complimented her childhood-self.

"Ach they are. They're our blessings from Gott. Noah and I prayed for a long time before we were blessed with our kinner. Do you have any kinner?" Lydia asked.

Celia shook her head. "Nee, not just yet. Frist, I have to find a mann."

Lydia chuckled as they reached the door. "That's the simple part. You pray for him and Gott sends him to you. Take my word for it. He sent me my Noah when I least expected it."

Celia smiled at the affection in her mother's voice. "Then I'll do just that, but first, let's get you to the doctor."

Lucas was already waiting for them on the porch. When Celia helped her mother outside, Celia noticed the concern in her brother's eyes. Her mother might have had trouble with her memory, even with her words but this was the first time she had trouble with mobility.

They silently shared the significance of this regression, both realizing that it might mean more than just another bad day.

Chapter 9
A Strong Foundation

On the first day of construction, Daniel was eager to begin. Lucas and Celia had made no changes to his plans, instead they had both embraced the idea of an open-floor plan and wide hallways. The addition of the mudroom and the large west-facing porch had been welcomed.

During the week it had taken Daniel to order the lumber and start planning his construction on the Eymann house, he had thought of Celia the whole time. His timeline, finishings, and even the grain of wood he had ordered for the floorboards had been with her in mind.

Daniel didn't allow himself to ponder too much on how strong his attraction for Celia was, although it came as a surprise. He thought of her even when he wasn't working. Before he climbed into bed at night, he envisioned her standing on the porch he had built, waving back at him with a smile.

The lumber had arrived the day before, which meant that Daniel could start working as soon as he arrived. He had arranged with Lucas to clear the area of brush and grass where the house would come and was pleased to see he had a clean canvas to start with on his arrival.

"Daniel, right on time," Lucas waved to him from the barn as he approached Daniel's buggy.

Daniel waved back. "Of course. If I want to be finished right on schedule, that means there's no room for tardiness."

Lucas smiled back at him, pleased with his words. "Ryan and I are off to the fields. Is there anything you need help with before we head off? Maybe help with off-loading your tools?"

"That would be gut, denke." Daniel appreciated the offer; one he didn't receive from most of his clients.

A short while later Daniel was surrounded by his tools, four sawhorses, and a table he always used to keep the plans open on. He pulled out his flask and poured himself a cup of coffee, ready to start his day.

Lucas and Ryan headed into the corn fields which were to be harvested over the next few weeks, leaving Daniel alone to start on his project.

As soon as his coffee was finished, he began, completely losing track of time as he measured and sawed the pieces of lumber that would be used as the foundation of the new home.

It was past lunch time when he caught sight of Celia for the first time. He had expected her to stop by through the duration of the morning, but to his disappointment, she hadn't come.

Now that he watched her nearing him, he felt his heart skip a beat with anticipation. She looked beautiful as ever, with the autumn breeze ruffling her hair, but her eyes looked tired.

"Guten mayrie, ach I'm sorry. I forgot it's afternoon already," Celia explained with a smile.

"Hullo Celia. Busy day?" Daniel questioned, wondering why her eyes seemed tired and her face seemed pale. Was she ill? He felt concern wash over him unexpectedly. He barely knew Celia, and yet he felt a strong need to protect and care for her.

"Jah, you could say that. Mamm had a rough morning. She argued with me the whole time," Celia admitted with a shrug.

"I can imagine it must be hard. How do you do it?" Daniel shook his head. "I'm sorry. I didn't mean to be intrusive."

Celia let out a heavy sigh. "I do it because I love her. And even if she doesn't remember who I am on days like today, I remember. I remember how she kissed my hurts, how she cuddled me in cold weather, and how she was patient when I was stubborn. It's just... She's forgetting more and more. This morning she thinks I'm an intruder in her haus. She keeps telling me she's going to tell Noah to call the police. The *Englisch Police!*"

"Ouch," Daniel flinched. The Amish hardly ever bothered the Englisch police with their problems, which made it so much worse. "Is she resting now?"

"Jah, I finally convinced her to take a nap. Hopefully when she wakes, she'll feel better," Celia explained looking at the piles of lumber behind him. "I still can't believe all these pieces of lumber are going to be my new haus."

"You better believe it. Do you see these, that have already been cut and measured? They'll be the supports for the foundation of the house. By the end of the day, I hope to have them in place and in concrete so they can set while I build the floor," Daniel explained.

"How far above the ground will the house be? I know it will be raised to protect it from flooding and snow," Celia asked, intrigued.

"Just three feet. That's enough to protect you against both. Since we're building a raised home, it also saves on the amount of concrete required for the foundation. But it means that the structure of the base and the floor needs to be more resilient and stronger than usual floors," Daniel explained.

Celia yawned and shook her head with an apology. "I'm sorry, you'll have to excuse my bad manners."

Daniel searched her gaze and sympathized. "Why don't you go lie down for a while as well? It's clear you're exhausted."

"Nee, I couldn't do that. I still have ironing to do and then there are the floors and I have to start on dinner..." Celia quickly explained.

"Celia, I'm sure your bruder and his frau would understand if you didn't get to the ironing and the floors. As for dinner, I'm sure you can start on it a little later for once. Go on, rest," Daniel encouraged her.

Celia looked at the lumber and the plans before she met his gaze again. "Denke for taking on this project at the last-minute, Daniel. I think once Mamm and I have a place of our own, it will be better for everyone."

"Only if you rest when she does. Taking care of her... I can imagine it's not only physically exhausting but mentally as well," Daniel probed gently.

"I don't mind," Celia insisted. "I better get back to work. I didn't mean to bother you," Celia said with a smile before she turned and headed back towards the house.

Daniel already knew she would not rest.

A sigh escaped him, wondering how he could help her. He knew that Lydia's condition wasn't one that would become better in the future, and he couldn't help but wonder if Celia's siblings realized how exhausted she was.

As he continued to saw the wood, he said a prayer for Celia. A prayer for strength, for rejuvenation of her soul, and a prayer of blessings for the unselfish way with which she cared for her mother.

Shortly after lunch time he had cut all the supports to length. Daniel set them in place and mixed the concrete that would keep them strong enough to support Celia's home. It was hard, labor intensive work that required a lot of energy.

Each hole was dug, a support inserted, and concrete poured around it. Once it was set, he would check the measurements again to make sure it would match up with the rest of the supports.

By the time the sun began its descent in the west, Daniel had placed twelve supports.

Pleased at the amount of work he had mastered on the first day, he packed up his things and headed home.

But not without glancing at the Eymann house and thinking about Celia again.

Chapter 10
Haunting Thoughts and Fears

"Celia, don't worry. Sarah will take gut care of Mamm while we're away," Lucas assured his sister as they drove into town.

The doctor had called the day before, explaining that he wanted to meet with all three of the Eymann siblings after receiving Lydia's latest test results. Ever since the doctor had called, Celia had an unsettling feeling come over her.

The doctor had never asked to meet with them without their mother, which could only mean one thing: what he had to say was something her mother could no longer comprehend, or something the doctor didn't want her mother to know.

"I know. She's just been a little difficult over the last few days," Celia explained, glancing at Daisy.

"Sarah will be fine, Mamm, as well. We have to be positive," Daisy insisted.

"I agree with Daisy," Lucas said as they drove into town.

Celia didn't argue with them, although she couldn't help but feel concerned. She had only ever left her mother with either Lucas or Daisy. It wasn't that she didn't trust her sister-in-law. It was merely a matter of not wanting to burden a woman six months into her pregnancy with her mother, who seemed confused almost all the time.

They walked into the clinic side by side. Both Lucas and Daisy following in Celia's footsteps, since Celia had been the one bringing her mother to appointments over the last few years.

When they arrived at his offices, his receptionist asked them to have a seat while she notified the doctor of their arrival.

Celia's hands were clammy from anxiety. She couldn't help but fear for the worst. She knew her mother's condition had deteriorated, but she was afraid to know just how much.

"Eymann family?" the doctor said, stepping into the reception area. "Come on back to my office."

Once they were all seated, the doctor opened the file in front of him and met Celia's questioning gaze. "The last time we did these tests to establish the rate of regression of your mother's disease, I explained to you it could change. She had an aggressive onset and has been more or less stable over the last three years with none to little change at all."

Celia nodded. "Jah, until the last few weeks."

"That's why I recommended we do the tests again. With the human brain we can guesstimate what it will do, but more often than not, it's simply that, it's a guess." The doctor seemed almost apologetic.

"So what does that mean? What do the latest tests say?" Daisy asked impatiently.

"Daisy, hush! Let the doctor speak," Lucas quickly chastened his younger sister.

"I wasn't sure of the results. To be honest, I was a little stunned by them. That's why I took a few days to get back to you. I had them looked over by another specialist in the field and unfortunately, he confirmed my diagnosis. It seems your mother's disease has taken a turn for the worse. The aggressiveness it has shown since the last tests is almost unprecedented. Although it's natural for early onset aggressive Alzheimer to be unpredictable, we at least hoped that her disease had slowed its progression over the last couple of years." The doctor stood up and placed a scan of Lydia's brain against a light box.

"This dark area on the PET scan is the one which we based our initial diagnosis." He pulled up another scan and turned to the siblings with apology in his eyes. "Based on her most recent PET scan, you can see how the disease has progressed. It's become more aggressive, rapidly impeding her ability to comprehend, communicate, recall, and soon will affect her ability to control her motor functions as will."

"What do we do now? Is there a different medication or perhaps a treatment we can sign her up for?" Daisy asked.

Celia bit back the tears that threatened to spill. She'd done enough research about her mother's disease to know what these results mean.

"Doctor, if you don't mind, can you explain to us what the next step is, or what these tests mean for her quality of life?" Lucas asked, trying to keep his voice clear of emotion.

The doctor glanced at Celia with empathy before explaining the stages to her siblings as he had explained to Celia before.

"Alzheimer's has been defined as having seven distinct stages. In most cases, these stages overlap, but here's a summary of how it works. Stage one and Stage two usually go undetected. They could begin years before anyone notices. At the end of stage two, memory loss and misplacing objects usually begin. When I diagnosed your mother, she was just progressing from leaving Stage three and entering Stage four. That means that she had forgotten names, places, and had trouble remembering plans. For the last two years, she has consistently remained in Stage four. She couldn't do simple tasks anymore; would forget which day of the week or what month it was. She couldn't cook anymore and had trouble remembering how to take care of herself. Sometimes she might have mistaken old memories for the current time–things like that."

"Jah, that's right," Celia agreed. "Which stage has she entered now?"

The doctor sighed heavily. "I'm sorry Celia, but it seems your mother has crossed briefly into Stage five and is now well into Stage six. The forgetfulness, frequent delusions, and confusion will only become more part of her daily life. Soon she might have trouble feeding or even dressing herself. You need to be prepared that it's only a matter of time before this might start happening."

"How long? A week, a month?" Daisy demanded.

"He can't say for sure," Celia explained on the doctor's behalf. "We'll just have to be patient and accept it when it happens." Celia turned to the doctor. "How long before she progresses into stage seven? I know you can't say for sure, but I need to know at least an estimate of how long we have…"

"What happens in stage seven?" Lucas asked.

"She wouldn't be able to care for herself at all. She'll need a permanent caregiver, someone knowledgeable and patient enough to help make her comfortable at the end," the doctor said quietly.

Silence hung over the doctor's room while all three of the Eymann children took a moment to mourn for what was to come. The doctor patiently waited until Lucas was the first to speak.

"Where do we find someone like that?" Lucas asked.

"Well, there are nurses for hire, hospice centers, there are quite a few options available. I can put you in touch with a social worker. It's natural for families to want the best for their loved ones during this final phase. Not everyone is equipped for caring for a loved one with end stage Alzheimer's."

"That won't be necessarily. I'll do it," Celia said firmly.

"Celia, you can't," Daisy argued.

Celia…" Lucas began, but Celia cut him off.

"I've been looking after Mamm since they diagnosed her. No one understands her needs or this illness better than me. I'm sure I'll need to learn a little more about helping her when she loses control of her motor functions, but I'm not afraid to learn. I'm doing this, with or without your approval." Celia had never heard her own voice sound so firm or so stubborn before in her life.

The doctor smiled at her with kindness. "I had a feeling that was what you would say. Some books might help you prepare. I've also made a list of things to look out for, when to call me and when to get her to an emergency room. If you change your mind Celia, you know no one will blame you?" the doctor asked as he slid the books along with a sheet of paper across the table towards Celia.

"I won't change my mind, denke doctor," Celia assured him. "I'll call you if I have questions."

"All right. Her new prescription is waiting for you at reception. It should help manage her confusion or at least keep her calm when she's having a delusion."

Together, they collected the prescription and when they finally returned to the buggy, Lucas stopped her from climbing in. "We don't expect this of you, Celia. You have your own life to live."

"I know you don't expect it, Lucas, but this is something I want to do," Celia explained. "I'm not blaming you or Daisy for not being willing. I understand you have your own families and babies on the way. But I don't. I want to do this for Mamm. Please don't stand in my way."

"Celia, we're just worried about you," Daisy added from the buggy.

"Don't be. I'll be fine, and with the new haus, it will be even more convenient to care for Mamm than it is now," Celia assured them. "Kumm, let's get back home."

No one said a word on the ride home. Each lost in their own thoughts and fears.

Chapter 11
Confidences with a Carpenter

Daniel arrived at the Eymann farm at first light and left for home when the light faded in the evenings. He had never been so dedicated or determined to get a project done with speed and efficiency as he was with Celia's house.

Daniel couldn't be sure if it was because he looked forward to catching glimpses of her during the day or if it was because when he saw her, she seemed tired and sad. Perhaps it was both, but somehow Daniel couldn't help but think that once her home was ready, she would be better.

His reasoning made little sense, but he didn't know what else he could do to make her look happy again.

He was just packing up the last of his tools when Lucas and Ryan returned from a day of harvesting. Ryan waved to him before he set off for the cottage he shared with Daisy. Lucas headed towards him.

"You're making gut progress, faster than I imagined," Lucas said, looking at the frame that was coming together bit by bit.

He had secured the foundation of the home with beams. The first sheets of flooring had been nailed into place during the day.

Daniel nodded. "Jah, from here you will see a little more progress until the roof is up, then things slow down again. The foundation part takes the longest—it's the most important part to get right."

Lucas nodded. "Jah, Daed always said if you plan on doing something, the first part is the most important. Ryan and I did the cottage for him and Daisy, but I have to say it wasn't nearly as neat or impressive as this."

"I'm sure it's just fine," Daniel smiled, knowing that Lucas was skilled enough. He just didn't have the time available at the moment.

"She'll want a mudroom when the boppli grows up," Lucas said with half a smile. "Sarah's already nagging about it as well."

"Then I'll help you with the plans when the time comes," Daniel nodded. He didn't mind helping where he could.

"I just hope this haus will make life easier for Celia…" Lucas said almost to himself.

Daniel didn't want to pry, but he could see Lucas was concerned about his sister. "With your mamm, you mean?"

"Jah. We went to see the doctor a few days ago… Mamm's regressed even more. Celia insists on caring for her. Daisy and I at least wanted to consider the option of a caretaker or a nurse, but Celia… she's stubborn." Lucas sighed heavily. "I'm worried about her. It's as if ever since Mamm got sick, Celia stopped living her own life. She spends every waking moment either taking care of Mamm or taking care of the haus for us. The more we tell her we don't expect her to, the more she insists it's the least she can do. She has even stopped attending her quilting group. That used to be her time to relax, to get out a little…" Lucas looked up and met Daniel's gaze. "Ach, I'm sorry Daniel. I'm sure you don't want to listen to me go off about our familye problems."

"I don't mind at all," Daniel said with understanding. Now it made sense why Celia had seemed so sad and tired over the last few days. "It must be hard on all of you, and I can understand you're concerned for Celia. Perhaps moving into her own place with your mamm is exactly what she needs. Her own space. She might feel less insistent about doing your haus chores."

"That's what we're hoping for," Lucas agreed. He shook his head in another sigh. "I don't feel guilty for finding Sarah and I can't blame Daisy for her happiness as well. I just wish the timing was different. Daisy and I have our families, with little ones on the way to balance the sadness of my mother's illness, but it's all Celia thinks about."

"Why don't you encourage her to go to her quilting group again? I'm sure Sarah or Daisy won't mind watching your mamm?" Daniel suggested, hoping he wasn't overstepping.

"We've tried. She doesn't even go into town to do the marketing anymore. She's become so protective of Mamm, as if she doesn't want to miss a single second with her," Lucas shrugged. "I can't even blame her. After what the doctor said…" Lucas trailed off, his gaze drifting to his harvested fields.

"Can I ask what the doctor said?" Daniel asked quietly.

"Of course. It's just… Mamm's had a setback. It's likely her disease will progress faster from here on out." Lucas's voice was gravelly with emotion.

"I'm very sorry to hear that, Lucas," Daniel sympathized. "If there's anything I can do, perhaps help with the chores to make things a little easier on Celia…"

"Denke. We'll all right for now, but I appreciate knowing that you're here during the day. Denke for the offer. I better get inside; it's getting late and supper is probably already on the table."

"Jah, I better get home," Daniel said, taking off his tool belt.

Lucas looked at him with curiosity for a moment before he smiled. "Join us for dinner. It's the least I can do after chewing off your ear with my troubles."

Daniel was about to decline when he found himself nodding. "Denke, I'd like that very much."

He'd like the opportunity to see Celia even more.

Chapter 12
More Than Meets The Eye

Celia set the dish with roast potatoes on the table just as Lucas came through the back door. "I asked Daniel to join us for dinner."

Celia's heart skipped a beat as she looked up to see the handsome carpenter standing behind her brother. "Hullo Daniel."

"Celia," Daniel nodded, taking off his hat. "The food smells delicious."

"Denke. It's just roast beef, potatoes, and carrots, I'm afraid. I ran a little late today," Celia quickly apologized for the limited variety of food on the table.

"We appreciate your trouble, either way," Sarah said by her side.

"Do you know where Noah is?" Lydia asked suddenly, looking straight at Daniel.

It caught Daniel off guard for a moment before he smiled at Celia's mother. "He'll be in shortly."

He wasn't sure if it was the right thing to say, but he didn't feel it was his place to inform her of her husband's passing. His answer earned him a silent thank you from Celia.

Everyone took their seats. Ryan and Daisy were dining at home tonight. They bowed their heads in silent prayer.

When Daniel's eyes opened, he found Celia watching with curiosity. A light blush colored her cheeks when she realized he had caught her. "Please help yourself, Daniel," Celia said quickly.

Daniel waited until Celia had served her mother before he helped himself to the food. As he ate, he couldn't help but be impressed by how tasteful the food was, considering how little time Celia had to cook now that her mother needed full time care.

"Ooof!" Sarah cried out before laughter bubbled from her throat. "This boppli keeps surprising me with his strength. I swear one of these days I'm going to have bruised ribs."

"He takes after his daed," Lucas said proudly.

Celia chuckled. "By the way, he's growing, you're not going to have enough room for him much longer."

"Luckily, I'm past the halfway mark," Sarah said gratefully, rubbing her side.

"It must be a wunderbaar feeling," Lydia said from her side of the table, a look of endearment and envy in her eyes.

Daniel didn't understand it since she'd carried three children. But he didn't question her either. Perhaps she was a little confused and forgot about it.

"It truly is," Sarah agreed, turning to Celia. "One day you'll experience it for yourself, and you'll understand that although you haven't even met this little person yet, he's already stolen your heart."

"Or her," Celia interjected with a smile. "Either way, he or she has already stolen my heart."

"Dinner was wunderbaar as always Celia," Lucas complimented her as he gathered the plates. "Why don't you join our guest for kaffe on the porch and leave Mamm and the dishes to me and Sarah?"

"Nee, I couldn't, possibly. You'll just end up being covered in soap suds and make even more work for Sarah," Celia teased.

Lucas shrugged. "Eventually, I'll have to accept helping a little more. It won't be long now before you have your own soap suds to worry about."

Daniel saw something cross in Celia's gaze before she smiled. "Denke, I wouldn't mind sitting outside for a bit."

Daniel helped Lucas gather the dishes while Sarah helped Lydia to her bedroom and Celia made them coffee. A few minutes later, they headed out to the porch, nothing but the sounds of the night surrounding him.

It was peaceful, the air just cool enough to go without a coat. Soon you wouldn't be able to sit outside without one, he thought as he sipped on his coffee.

"I can't believe the haus it taking shape so quickly. I thought it would take much longer," Celia said as the moonlight cast light over her new home.

"Wait until the walls go up, then it feels like it's magically being built over night," Daniel said, turning to her with a smile. "Do you like it so far?"

"Very much!" Celia agreed, smiling right at him. Why was it that when she was with Daniel, it felt as if the heavy weight on her shoulders seemed to disappear? It was as if for a few moments she was just Celia.

She wasn't a sister, a daughter, or anything anyone else needed.

Just Celia.

"Dinner was very nice. You're a gut cook. I never knew that about you," Daniel complimented her, wanting to hold on to the magic of the moment.

Celia felt her smile broaden even more. "If you think that's gut, you haven't tasted my chicken fried steak yet. Daisy swears it's the best in the entire world."

Daniel's laughter was deep, making chill travel down her spine. Something about him made her aware of things she'd never even noticed before.

She had picked up on the few lines around his eyes, just like the one crooked tooth that graced his smile. Celia had noticed the cadence of his voice changed when he spoke to her, just like his smile seemed more tender.

There was something here between them, something she couldn't name.

But it was something she wanted to explore.

"Perhaps you'll invite me for dinner again?" Daniel asked with a hopeful smile.

Celia searched his gaze and realized she wouldn't mind spending more time with Daniel. She couldn't remember much of him as a child, but Daniel, as a man, intrigued her very much.

She wanted to learn everything about him. Why he'd gone into construction when his father had turned to the furniture side of carpentry.

"I didn't mean to impose by saying that," Daniel said quickly.

Celia shook her head. "Not at all. Actually, I was just wondering why you went into construction and not follow your daed's footsteps with the furniture."

Daniel leaned back and crossed his legs at his ankles. "I've thought of that quite a few times over the years. To be honest, I can't answer it myself. I think... perhaps it's because I don't want my creations to be part of a home. I want it to be the home... if that makes sense? I enjoy bringing something to life from nothing. Giving people more space to live, giving them the freedom of turning their haus into a functional home."

"Well, my haus is certainly functional. I would've never thought of raising it for the snow and floods. And the mudroom... I've already thought of using it as a greenhouse as well. I could grow my seedlings there through the winter so that they're ready for replanting in the summer."

"That's a very gut idea," Daniel smiled at her. "You seem to have a lot of those."

Celia laughed softly. "Sometimes. But as of late, I have had little time to have any ideas at all." She glanced back over her shoulder towards the door before she turned to Daniel again. "Mamm's been demanding a little more of my time."

She wouldn't tell Daniel how exhausted she was, or how afraid she was. She couldn't reveal her deepest fears to anyone, not even to her siblings. A caretaker would help so much with the responsibility, but Celia refused to see her mother as a chore that needed to be checked off a list. She didn't have a family or a job outside of the home that demanded her attention. The least she could do was give her mother all the attention she needed.

"You're a selfless woman, Celia Eymann. A woman to admire," Daniel whispered.

Their gazes met and Celia felt her heart swell. Her siblings had thanked her so often for helping with her mother, but to have someone else compliment her for it... it nearly brought tears to her eyes.

"Denke Daniel," Celia finally said when she'd got her cracked voice under control.

"It's true. I've seen how much you do, Celia. You deserve to rest now and then as well. Like I suggested the other day..." Daniel encouraged.

Celia shook her head. "There simply isn't time. Besides, we can rest when we reach the heavenly gates. I can't imagine any of us giving my mamm any rest when we were younger."

Daniel laughed. "True enough. Between Daisy and Lucas, your mamm had to be on her toes all the time. Except with you... you've always been quiet and disciplined."

Celia chuckled. "Really? That's your description of me?"

"I don't know you well enough to have another one," Daniel said simply.

Celia was quickly reminded of how little time she'd spent away from her mother over the last few months. She pushed the thought aside and turned to Daniel with a smile. "Perhaps you'll get to know me better while you're building my haus."

"I look forward to it," Daniel said with a hopeful smile.

Celia's heart skipped another beat, realizing she did as well.

"Denke for dinner. I've got to be on my way, but I'll see you tomorrow?" Daniel asked, standing up.

Celia nodded. "I'm always here, if you haven't noticed."

"I've noticed… more than just that," Daniel finished a little quietly. "Gut night, Celia."

Celia waved Daniel off and watched his buggy disappear into the darkness. She wasn't sure what he had meant by that, but it made her heart feel light and happy.

Just perhaps, Daniel was watching her from his construction site whenever he had a second free, just like Celia had been watching him from the windows whenever she had a minute.

Chapter 13
Research and Romance

Daniel leaned back in the chair in the library and let out a quiet sigh.

Ever since Lucas had told him about his concern for Celia, Daniel had become more and more concerned as well. When they had enjoyed coffee on the porch, Daniel had realized that his attraction for Celia wasn't just curiosity. There was much more between them than he had realized at first.

There was something stronger, almost magnetic pulling him towards her.

Over the last few days, he had made a point of walking over to her whenever she was outside. Whether he kept her company while she was hanging out laundry or asked her about her day while she swept the porch, he enjoyed talking to her either way.

He looked forward to the small breaks in his day, but he wanted to understand more about what she was dealing with with her mother. Daniel tried to be sympathetic, but how could he really understand when all he knew about the disease was what he had learned from Celia and her siblings?

Not wanting to burden them with the questions, or making them feel as if he was intruding, Daniel left the

Eymann farm early today. But instead of going home, he had stopped at the library in town.

Daniel had spent many hours in the library reading about construction. He respected the written word, and today was no different. After two hours of reading, the information he had learned overwhelmed him.

To Daniel, Alzheimer's had always just been a disease of the old. A disease of confusion and forgetfulness that came with age. But now he realized although it affected the elderly more, it could affect anyone over the age of forty.

They had diagnosed Lydia young, but her early onset aggressive Alzheimer's was scarcer and trickier to deal with. There weren't specific timelines or treatments to help with the progression of her disease.

Instead, there was only patience.

After learning more about Lydia's disease and what Celia had to deal with daily, he respected her even more. His heart ached for her, knowing that if her mother's disease had already progressed to mobility problems, the road was only going to be harder from here. He couldn't help but wish there was something he could do for her.

Daniel couldn't imagine having one of his own parents going through what Lydia was suffering through. Even more concerning than caring for a parent suffering from the disease was realizing you could one day suffer from it as well.

No wonder Celia was sad and tired.

She was witnessing what could be her future.

Daniel closed the book and decided that Celia needed more than a friend. Celia needed someone who understood, someone to whom she could talk. She had become a pillar of support for her siblings.

But who supported Celia?

Daniel left the library, deciding that he would become that pillar for her. Although his interest in her was much more than just becoming a friend, Daniel would support her either way. Celia didn't have time to visit with her friends, or to talk to anyone but her siblings, but now she would have him.

He would be there for her on the hard days and he would celebrate the good days with her. He couldn't even blame her for not having a beau. How could she focus on falling in love or being courted when the constant weight of her mother's illness, along with the fear of what the future might hold, was constantly haunting her?

That evening, Daniel kneeled before his bed and prayed to the Lord that he could be what Celia needed. That he could be her strength, her happiness and most of all that he could be the person she turned to when life became too hard.

Daniel knew she wouldn't turn to her siblings.

Celia would never admit her fears to her siblings; not because she didn't trust them to console her, but because she wanted to be the one consoling them.

As always, Celia was selfless to a point.

But now, at least she would have him, Daniel promised himself, before he fell asleep.

Chapter 14
Bad Timing

Celia set the iced tea down on the porch before she waved to Daniel where he was hammering nails into a wall.

Her heart fluttered when Daniel waved back.

It had been almost six weeks since they had seen her mother's doctor, and it was as if Celia could notice the regression every single day. Her moments of clarity were further and further apart and when she had them, they were only for a short period. Whenever she stepped outside, it was as if Daniel appeared magically to be there for her.

Celia wasn't sure when or how it happened, but over the last few weeks, Daniel had become a part of her life. It had started with small chats here and there and had progressed to him being there when she needed a shoulder, a helping hand, or simply someone to sit with her while she processed her mother's latest delusion.

Although she couldn't dare to think about anything but her mother at the moment, Celia hoped that in the future she might have time to explore the connection she shared with Daniel.

As Daniel walked over to the porch, Celia took in her new home. The walls were up, and the roof was already in place. Daniel was now erecting the inside walls. It was as if her dream of having a home of her own was coming to life right before her eyes, even as she realized she was losing her mother.

The only mother she'd only ever loved.

"How was she this morning?" Daniel asked as he joined her on the porch.

Celia let out a heavy sigh. "It was a hard morning."

"Want to talk about it?" Daniel asked kindly.

Celia turned to him and searched his empathetic gaze. "I feel bad dumping all of my complaints on you. It feels as if it's all I ever do."

Daniel chuckled. "I feel honored. Tell me," Daniel reached for her hand.

Celia's heart stopped for a moment. It was the first time Daniel had done something of the kind. She looked at their hands before her gaze met his.

"I care Celia," Daniel said simply. "I want to be there for you; let me."

Celia swallowed past the lump in her throat. She knew Daniel meant it; he wasn't just saying it to appease her. Letting out a sigh, she told him about her morning and how her mother refused to get dressed. She explained to him how Lydia had refused to eat before she asked Celia to leave.

After telling Daniel everything, only keeping to herself that her mother's incontinence was weighing heavily on her mind, she let out a sigh. "Tomorrow will be a gut day again," Celia said hopefully.

"I'm sure it will," Daniel squeezed her hand. "I just can't imagine how hard it must be for you to watch her go through this knowing that… that it might happen to you or your siblings one day."

Celia had never even thought of that. Since they were adopted the hereditary factor of her mother's disease hadn't even occurred to her. She had told no one about her adoption, only her siblings knew. But as she sat on the porch with Daniel holding her hand, Celia wanted to share it with him.

"I… Lucas, Daisy, and I won't be affected. We learned a couple of years ago that we were adopted."

Daniel's eyes widened for a moment with surprise before his gaze softened. "How did you feel when you learned about that? I take it you didn't know?"

"Nee, none of us knew. It was in the early days of Mamm's disease. She let something slip to Lucas… he figured it out. Honestly…" Celia thought for a moment. "I haven't given it much thought. I don't think it really matters. I believe Gott put us exactly where he wanted us to be. He wanted me to be raised by Lydia and Noah. He wanted me to care for Lydia. My birth parents… I'll never know their reasons for giving me up, but I'll forever be grateful to them. This is where I belong."

"Celia…" Daniel trailed off, shaking his head. "I don't know how to say this, but I'm going to try. I know you don't have time, and I know you're occupied with your mamm, but I wish to spend more time with you. Everything about you… you're an amazing woman."

Celia's mouth curved into a smile. Until now, Daniel had only been a friend. But to hear him say the words, to clarify that he liked her. That he also felt what she felt… made her day a little brighter. "I also wish we could spend more time together."

"Perhaps one day..." Daniel mused with a hopeful smile. "But until then... I'm here for you. Always. If you need to shout, cry, or laugh, or just a shoulder to lean on, I'm here for you, Celia."

Celia's heart swelled in her chest. "And what do you get in return? I can't offer you anything Daniel, I don't even have time for friends or my quilting group. I can't even remember the last time I attended Sunday service."

Daniel smiled warmly before he winked at her. "I get the pleasure of your company. That's more than enough for me."

Celia laughed, already feeling lighter than she had when she had stepped out onto the porch. "Denke, Daniel. I have to check on her."

"And I have to finish building your haus," Daniel said, standing up.

Their gazes met and held for a moment, both having so much they wanted to say but both knowing that the timing wasn't right.

When Daniel finally broke away and headed towards the house he was building, Celia quietly prayed that one day timing would be in their favor.

Chapter 15
When the Fog Lifts

"There was a storm, the thunder was so loud!" Lydia said in the voice of a little girl instead of the adult woman that she was.

Celia shifted onto the bed and wrapped an arm around her mother. "It's all right, it was just a bad dream."

She had woken up before Lucas or Sarah from her mother's anxious cries. It was a little after two in the morning as Celia had tip-toed to her mother's bedroom. Her mother's face was covered with cold sweat, her eyes wide with fear from the nightmare that had seemed so real.

"Daed was in the barn... the barn the storm took..." Lydia wept quietly for the father she had lost over five decades ago.

This was the hardest part, Celia realized. Watching her mother relive losses from years ago, repeatedly. It broke her heart every time. Celia quietly wept as she held onto her mother, waiting for her mother to calm down.

"It's all right, Mamm, there isn't a storm. See, the sky is clear. We can almost see the stars if we look closely," Celia said, pointing to the window.

Her mother sniffed back her tears and turned her head to the window. "There isn't a storm?"

"Nee, just a bad dream from when you were a little girl. The tornado that took your daed... it was a long time ago. You're safe now." Celia continued to console her mother.

She waited until her mother had stopped shaking before she moved and sat beside her. "There, better now?"

Lydia frowned and narrowed her eyes as she searched Celia's face. Her hand reached out and stroked Celia's cheek. "I know you..."

Celia nodded with a sad smile. She wouldn't get her hopes up. Her mother's moments of lucidity were so rare these days. "Jah, you know me. Do you know who I am?"

Celia held her breath, wishing for just a few minutes of clarity. Just a few seconds with the woman she used to know.

Lydia's eyes filled with tears again. "Celia... My Celia... Ach what a beautiful woman you've become. Noah would've been so proud."

It was as if the fog had lifted and Lydia's eyes were clear, as was her mind.

Celia swallowed back the tears of joy. "Jah Mamm, it's me."

"How have you been? It feels like I haven't seen you in ages..." Lydia sighed. "It's the disease, isn't it?"

Celia didn't answer. She simply nodded. "Lucas and Daisy are both expecting their first kinner."

Lydia's face beamed. "Ach, how wunderbaar to blessed with kinner. It was a wish of mine that was never granted. But Gott blessed me even more when he gave the three of you to me." Lydia smiled wryly. "I can still remember the first time I laid eyes on each of you... it was as if we were meant to be."

"Ich liebe dich Mamm," Celia said, biting back the tears. She didn't want to ruin this moment of clarity with tears.

"I love you too my dochder. I'm so sorry I never told you about your adoption. Not being able to bear kinner felt like a failure to me. I was so afraid your daed would blame me... But when we got you... I never once thought of you as someone else's—that's why I didn't think to tell you. Can you ever forgive me?" Lydia asked, grasping both of Celia's hands.

Celia nodded. "There's nothing to forgive. You're the only mamm I ever had. You're my mamm, regardless of what a piece of paper might say. We might not be blood, but we're bonded by heart."

Lydia hugged Celia tightly before she leaned back and framed her face again. "What about you? Do you have kinner yet?"

Celia chuckled and shook her head. "Nee Mamm, I've been... busy."

"Finding a mann hopefully?" Lydia teased.

In moments like these, it was hard to accept that her mother was ill. It was as if they had never diagnosed her at all. "Not just yet."

"You should, Celia. Finding the right mann is almost as precious as holding your first boppli. It's a kind of connection, a kind of love you can't explain to anyone—not until you experience it for yourself. You deserve the happiness, the peace and the joy that comes with that feeling," Lydia urged her.

"Mamm, I don't want to waste my time looking for a mann. I want to spend my time with you," Celia admitted tearfully.

Lydia clucked her tongue. "You've cared for me all this time… isn't it time you left the caring to someone else? No one would blame you, least of all I, if you found someone to take care of me…"

"Nee Mamm!" Celia insisted. "I'm taking care of you. Lucas and Daisy help. We're not letting anyone else take care of you."

"You always were stubborn. Stubborn, kind, and so gentle. I pray Gott sends you a gut mann, Celia," Lydia said with a warm smile.

Celia smiled and thought of Daniel. "I'll pray for the same."

Her mother frowned and glanced around the room. When her gaze met Celia's again, Celia knew before she spoke that their moment had ended. "Where's Noah?"

"He's checking on the horses. He'll be back any minute now. Why don't you try to rest?" Celia encouraged, struggling to keep the emotion out of her voice.

"I am tired. Please tell him not to take long," Lydia said sleepily as she lay down and let out a yawn.

"I will," Celia promised. Instead of returning to her room, Celia made herself comfortable in the rocking chair beside her mother's bed. She draped a blanket over her knees, wanting to be close if her mother had another nightmare.

Perhaps if she was lucky, it would bless her with another moment of clarity.

Chapter 16
Things To Be Done

Celia woke from the sun teasing her eyelids as the rays filtered in through the window. She only had to glance outside to know that she'd overslept. She yawned before shoving the blanket aside that she had draped over her legs.

Her back was stiff from sleeping in the rocking chair, her upper body ice-cold. She stood up and stretched before glancing back at the bed. Her mother's figure was unmoving as she slept. Relieved that her mother hadn't had another nightmare, Celia went in search of coffee.

She found Lucas and Sarah in the kitchen, sharing breakfast. "Guten mayrie."

"Guten mayrie. We thought we'd leave you, you seemed so peaceful," Lucas explained. "Did Mamm have a hard night?"

Celia poured herself a cup of coffee. "Jah, she had a nightmare about the tornado that took her daed."

"Ach nee, she must have been terribly upset," Sarah sympathized. "Why didn't you wake me? I would've helped."

Celia shook her head. "She calmed down quickly. She was lucid. Lucas, it was the most lucid I've seen her in weeks. She apologized for not telling us about the adoptions. She's so excited for the babies that are coming..." Celia smiled at the memory.

"That must have been worth waking up for," Lucas returned her smile.

"I better go wake her. If she sleeps in too long, she'll be confused with her routine for most of the day," Celia said, turning to Lucas. "Will you brew her tea?"

"Of course," Lucas agreed, standing up.

Celia had a smile on her face as she returned to her mother's bedroom. The few moments they had shared the night before had meant more to Celia than she could ever explain. It gave her hope that there would be more. The moments of clarity might be few, but when they did occur, it was like witnessing the first rays of sun falling on a frozen lake in winter.

It was spectacular.

Celia touched her mother's shoulder. "Mamm, time to wake up, sleepy head."

When her mother didn't move, Celia tried again. "Kumm Mamm, your tea is getting cold."

The mention of tea always roused her mother, but it didn't earn a single reaction now. Feeling slightly concerned, Celia brushed a hand over her mother's hair.

Her heart stopped realizing her mother was cold. She slowly slid her hand from her mother's hair to her forehead. Her heart didn't resume beating, instead it exploded with such pain that for a moment Celia thought she might be having a heart attack.

She gasped for breath, struggling to call out for Lucas. Tears burst from her eyes even as it robbed her of her breath. She finally cried out for her brother in ragged tones.

Lucas rushed into the room, but stopped as soon as he saw Celia. Celia didn't know what to say or what to do. She just shook her head and continued to cry.

Lucas moved to her side. He wrapped his big, brawny arms around her and held her as she wept. Neither of them said a word as they sat by Lydia's bed, weeping for a life just departed.

A short while later, Sarah came to see what was the matter. She had barely stepped into the room before she gasped. "I'll call for Daisy."

"She was fine. She wasn't sick… How…" Celia asked into her brother's chest. "It just makes little sense… We were talking…"

"Hush, it's all right," Lucas said, rubbing her back. "The doctor warned us this could happen. He warned us she could stop breathing, or that her heart could stop beating."

"Not this soon… he didn't say it could happen this soon!" Celia cried, struggling to accept the reality.

"He didn't know, schweschder. No one did. Only Gott knows when it's our time…" Lucas held her, giving her time to grieve.

By the time Daisy and Ryan arrived, Celia had finally caught her breath. The sight of her mother made her feel as if something inside her had left as well. Something she could never get back.

Celia stood up and gave Daisy and Lucas a moment alone to grieve, knowing there were things that needed to be done. She stepped into the kitchen and glanced at Ryan. "Could you please call an ambulance and the bishop?"

Ryan nodded and headed to the phone shanty.

Celia found a pad of paper and a pencil and made a list. If she was going to get through this day at all, she would need to keep busy.

"Celia, that can wait…" Sarah said, laying a hand on her shoulder.

Celia shook her head. "There are things that need to be done. The sooner they're dealt with, the sooner we can lay Mamm to rest."

Sarah knew better than to argue. Instead she made Celia another cup of coffee.

Chapter 17
Dust to Dust

If Celia thought that losing her father had been hard, she had been wrong. As she stood over her mother's grave, it felt as if a part of her had departed along with her mother through the heavenly gates.

Noah and Lydia Eymann might not have been her parents by birth, but they had been her everything. They had taught her right from wrong; they had supported her, believed in her, and had always been there for her.

Even when her mother had been diagnosed, she had firmly believed that they would at least have another ten years with her before they had to say farewell. Instead, they had only had three years and seven months.

The doctor, the bishop, and the entire community had sympathized with their sudden loss, but their sympathies didn't make it any easier to deal with. The only consolation was knowing that her mother wouldn't suffer any further. She wouldn't be reduced to a wheelchair, adult diapers, or being fed like a child.

It was relieving for Celia to know that her mother had passed with her dignity still intact. It was even more of a consolation that she had shared such a special moment with her mother only hours before her passing.

She would never forget the moment.

As the bishop said the final words at her mother's grave, Celia remembered her mother's words.

"Finding the right mann is almost as precious as holding your first boppli. It's a kind of connection, a kind of love you can't explain to anyone—not until you experience it for yourself. You deserve the happiness, the peace and the joy that comes with that feeling."

She had never felt more alone than in that moment. On her one side Lucas stood with Sarah, now eight months pregnant, with Sarah's familye standing behind them in a show of support.

On her other side, Daisy and Ryan stood, Ryan holding his wife's hand to support her.

Between them, Celia stood alone. She had no one she could call her own beside her, no family of loved ones behind her.

For the first time she realized she had been so focused on her mother than now that she was gone, Celia had no one.

Her breath caught at the realization, hating the thought that she no longer had her mother to care for. What would she do with her time? At least when she'd been taking care of her mother, she had a reason to live in Lucas's home. Now she didn't even have a reason to be there.

Celia felt her heart sting with pain, not only the loss but the realization of how bleak her future had become, when suddenly she felt a warm hand settle on her back. Surprised, she turned and looked right into Daniel's gaze.

He didn't need to say a single word. His eyes spoke for him. *I am here. You're not alone. I've got you.*

Celia had never appreciated any gesture more. She smiled at him weakly before she turned her attention back to the bishop.

"Ashes to ashes, dust to dust. May her soul rest in peace with our heavenly father. Amen."

One by one members of the community moved away from the grave. They would all be heading to Lucas's home for the sympathy tea. But Celia wasn't ready to go just yet.

Over the last few days, she had made certain that everything was in place for the funeral. They had arranged the sympathy tea; the refreshments and snacks all ready for the guests that would arrive.

Celia just needed another moment to say goodbye.

"We'll go welcome the guests," Lucas said, touching Celia's shoulder. He and Daniel shared a look before he turned and led Sarah to their buggy.

"Do you want me to stay with you?" Daisy asked, turning to Celia.

Celia shook her head. "Nee, I won't be long. You go on ahead."

Daisy and Ryan also headed to their buggy, leaving Celia and Daniel alone.

Celia let out a quiet sigh. "Gut bye Mamm, send my love to Daed."

Daniel slipped a hand around her shoulder and quietly offered support while she wept. Celia wasn't sure how long she stood there, but by the time she turned and met Daniel's gaze she knew it had been a while.

"I'm ready now," Celia said, wiping her eyes.

"Take all the time you need," Daniel said kindly. "I'm in no hurry."

Celia nodded gratefully. "Denke, for being here. For staying… for everything."

Daniel had helped where he could with the funeral arrangements. He'd even insisted on building her mother's casket at his own cost.

"I wouldn't have had it any other way." Daniel frowned and shook his head. "I wasn't planning on our first buggy ride to be like this, but… can I give you a ride home?"

Celia smiled wryly. "I'd appreciate it."

They rode in silence, Celia lost in her grief and mentally preparing herself for the onslaught of sympathy waiting for her at home. Daniel held her hand the entire way.

When they finally stopped in front of the barn between the myriad of buggies and children playing, Daniel turned to her with a concerned look. "If it becomes too overwhelming, find me. I'll help you leave."

Celia smiled at him with a doubting look. "I wish I could escape, but this is something I need to do."

"Then I'll be there with you every step of the way," Daniel promised.

With Daniel by her side, Celia felt stronger.

Strong enough to contain her emotions until the very last guest left, but not strong enough just yet to admit how much he meant to her.

She saw him out as a friend and went to bed an orphan.

Chapter 18
Silence Is Golden

"If you scrub that porch one more time, I'm going to have to replace it," Daniel said with a smile, filled more with concern than with humor.

Ever since Lydia's passing, he watched from a distance how Celia was working her fingers, literally, to the bone. It was as if she refused to let her hands be idle, for when she did, she grieved for her mother.

Daniel kept just enough distance to keep an eye on her, checked in on her at least once a day. As an outsider, he could see how Lydia's death had affected all the Eymann siblings. Daisy and Ryan mourned on their own, hardly coming by Lucas's home for dinner anymore.

Lucas had become quiet. His jaw clenched most of the time, as if he refused to allow himself to grieve. Sarah spent more time at the social services in town, either to make up for the time she would lose when the baby came, or to keep herself from being reminded of the loss.

Which left Celia mostly alone at home.

Alone with the memories, the heartache, and most of all, her thoughts.

Daniel didn't want to overwhelm her with sympathy, but he also didn't want to lose her to her grief. So now and then, like now, he would approach her as if she were an injured wild animal that needed tenderness but firmness as well. Celia needed to deal with her mother's passing and realize that she still had her own life to live.

She looked up from where she was scrubbing the porch. "There's no such thing as too clean a porch."

Daniel shrugged and leaned against the post. "That might be true, but there is such a thing as too much work?"

Celia frowned at him, clearly agitated by his interference.

"When's the last time you ate, Celia?" Daniel asked, softening his tone.

"What? How is that any of your concern?" Celia snapped with a temper he didn't know she had.

Daniel wasn't about to back off. He cared about her too much to let her drive him away when she needed him most. "Because I care. Because you've done nothing but clean and wash and work since... Because I can't stand seeing you like this..." Daniel finished, not knowing what else to say.

Celia dropped the brush in the bucket and stood up, her hands on her hips. "I didn't ask you to care about how I look."

Daniel let out a sigh of frustration. "You think I care how you look? I don't care in the least. It's your heart I care about. You're avoiding your grief and by doing it, it's affecting your health. You've lost weight, you're not sleeping, and don't even try to tell me you're not spending every waking moment scrubbing, cleaning, or fixing something that doesn't need to be cleaned or fixed."

Celia opened her mouth to argue, but stopped before she said a single word.

Daniel saw the tears fill her eyes even before the first one escaped. He rushed onto the porch and pulled her into his arms and held her as the tidal wave of grief overwhelmed her. She shook in his arms, her breaths coming in ragged pants as she struggled for air through the tears.

Daniel didn't let go of her once.

He felt her body grow heavy against his as her strength finally gave way.

Daniel helped her into one of the porch chairs and looked at her with sympathy. "I'm going to fetch us some tea."

She didn't even argue, instead, she just nodded.

When Daniel returned, the tears were gone. But now her eyes seemed empty. As if there was nothing left to feel, nothing left to live for. He handed her the cup and waited for her to break the silence.

"I don't know what else to do. Ever since I've been an adult, I took care of someone. First it was Lucas and Daisy, and then Mamm... without taking care of someone, I feel... lost. Without Mamm, I feel lost," Daisy admitted in barely more than a whisper.

"You're not lost. You're just feeling that way now because you're still dealing with the loss. It will take time, but it will get better," Daniel encouraged her. "Have you considered taking care of yourself for a change? All this time, all these years–who took care of you?"

"There was nothing wrong with me. I didn't need to be taken care of," Celia quickly turned to him with a frown.

"Everyone needs to be taken care of, Celia. Even if it's a just a cup of kaffe in the morning or a slight gesture... we all need to feel that we're cared for," Daniel corrected her.

"How do I do that? Daniel, you're confusing me," Celia said impatiently.

Daniel chuckled. "It's easy. For a few hours every day, do something just for yourself. Not because someone expects it, or because you feel it needs to be done. Something you want to do just because *you* want to."

"Like what?" Celia asked, perplexed.

"Like going to your quilting group again. Like taking an afternoon nap. Like weeping for your mamm when it seems the grief is going to overwhelm you. Take a walk, take a buggy ride, go to town; anything you want. As long as it's something you're doing because *you* want to do it," Daniel explained.

Celia thought for a long moment and sighed heavily. "Without having to take care of Mamm, it feels like I'm a burden to Lucas and Sarah..."

"That's not true, and you know that. That is all in your mind. It's time you get some fresh air and allow the cobwebs to be blown away," Daniel teased.

Celia laughed weakly. "Perhaps."

She tilted her head and searched his gaze. "Why are you so concerned about me?"

Daniel reached for her hand and held it. Now wasn't the time to tell her he'd fallen in love with her, or that he was waiting for her to deal with her grief before he courted her, but he could tell her something else. "Because I care."

Celia smiled, but didn't ask him to elaborate. Perhaps because she wasn't ready to hear what he meant by it, or perhaps because she understood he wasn't ready to tell her.

They sat like that until their tea turned cold.

Without saying a word, hand in hand, just knowing that it was enough that they were there together.

When Celia finally turned to him almost an hour later, her smile was peaceful. "Denke, I needed that. I needed to sit with someone without having to fill the silence with words."

Daniel smiled. "See, you did it. You did something because you wanted to."

Celia nodded with a grin. "Denke Daniel."

"Denke, I think I needed it as well." Daniel turned and headed back to work on the house.

For the rest of the afternoon, as he lay the floorboards on the porch, he wondered if it was too far-fetched of dreaming of sitting with Celia on that very porch in the future. He smiled as he worked, hoping that future wasn't too far away.

Chapter 19
Sunset Buggy Rides

At first, it had felt strange doing what she wanted. It had felt as if she were betraying Lucas and Sarah by not cleaning or cooking for them.

But after a heartfelt conversation with Lucas, Celia finally understood that he was concerned about her as well. He had the farm, Daisy had the school, both distractions that helped them deal with their grief.

Celia didn't.

Just like Daniel, Lucas insisted she take her time to find her own routine. He assured her she wasn't a burden and asked her instead if he could pay her a weekly wage for doing the housekeeping for him and Sarah. Celia insisted it wasn't necessary. Sarah, almost due, insisted it was since she could hardly do anything herself.

Between doing the housekeeping for Sarah and Lucas, Celia looked forward to spending an hour over lunch time sitting under the oak tree in her new yard while she talked to Daniel. He had become so much more than a friend to her, but Celia wasn't sure how to let him know how she felt.

Being caught up with her mother's care for such a long time, Celia had lost a little of her self-confidence, fearing that if she revealed her feelings to Daniel, she might frighten him away. Instead, she cherished the time they spent together.

They talked about everything and anything. From the finishing touches of her house, that was almost finished, right down to their faith. Both bittersweet for Celia. She couldn't wait to move into her own home, especially since it hurt to see her mother's room converted into a nursery for Lucas's baby that would make its arrival soon. But at the same it hurt to know that she had planned to live there with her mother, and now she would live there alone.

With her faith, it was hard to find peace with losing her mother. At times, she felt angry at Gott for taking her so soon, and at other times, she felt grateful that it spared her mother more suffering.

She learned that grief wasn't just an uphill battle, it was a mountain range filled with valleys and peaks. Some days you would reach a peak and move out of the depths of your despair and other days, it overshadowed you in a valley, unsure how you will ever reach the next peak.

Grief for Celia was a journey, not an overnight miracle cure of an open wound. She accepted that as well.

Celia had ventured into town to do the weekly marketing. At first, she had felt guilty for driving around when she could've found something to do at home. But by now she felt brave enough to return to her quilting group.

Today was the first time in two years she stood with her quilting basket in hand, ready to join a group of friends for an afternoon of quilting and tea. They welcomed her with open arms, sympathies once again pledged for losing her mother. For a few moments, Celia wasn't sure coming had been the right decision at all.

But as soon as the conversation turned to mild gossip, toddler milestones, and the best way to clean a wooden floor, Celia realized this was exactly where she needed to be. Only now did it occur to her how small her world had become, how focused her life had become around her mother.

With the clarity of hindsight, Celia knew that this new life was what she needed. She needed to listen to her friends complain about a sleepless night with colicky babies. She needed to laugh as one woman told about her husband's persistent snoring.

By the time the quilting bee ended, Celia felt rejuvenated and more than a little happy that she had come.

"It was so gut to have you Celia. Promise you'll come next week?" the hostess asked as Celia said goodbye.

Celia answered without hesitation. "Next week and the week after that, and every week after that. I forgot how much I needed this quilting group; I won't ever forget again."

"Gut, gut. It keeps us ferhoodled women sane," the hostess joked.

Celia laughed as she walked to her buggy. The sun was already halfway through its descent, but Celia didn't feel rushed by time at all. Sarah would cook dinner; Lucas would sit with her in the kitchen. Celia didn't have to rush home or worry about her mother, instead she could take her time driving home and if she felt like it, she could stop and watch the sunset and spare a thought for her mother.

She did just that.

Chapter 20
Early Birds &
Glass Houses

Celia brushed down her horse and gave him extra sugar cubes as a reward for waiting while she watched the sunset. Dusk had fallen over Lancaster County and the scent of horse, hay, and lumber mingled on the evening breeze as Celia walked out of the barn.

To her left, her new home stood proud, only a week or two away from being finished. Until now, she had been curious to see what it looked like inside, but she hadn't yet had the courage to look.

It still hurt to know that she wouldn't be sharing the excitement of moving into her new home with her mother.

But when the time came, Celia knew she would be just fine. Her mother would've wanted her to be.

She crossed the yard and glanced at the oak tree that stood in her yard. Lucas and Ryan had spent the last week putting up a fence around her yard, something Celia didn't understand. Was it to keep Lucas's kinner out when they were older, or perhaps to allow her to keep something in, like a chicken or a puppy?

Her mouth curved at the thought of getting a puppy, something to care for.

A soft chuckle escaped her as she reached the back door. Not now, but perhaps in a few months' time she would be ready to care for a puppy. A mischievous puppy that would chew on everything and destroy her yard. One that she would need to house train and discipline.

One that would become her companion.

"There you are. We've been waiting for you," Sarah said the moment Celia stepped through the door.

"I'm sorry I lost track of time. I stopped on my way back from the quilting bee and watched the sunset," Celia said, not feeling guilty at all.

"That sounds nice," Lucas commented. "Come on, we've got something we want to show you."

Celia frowned. "I thought I was late for dinner."

"Dinner can wait," Sarah urged Celia out the backdoor again.

Together, they walked towards Celia's new home. Celia's heart raced with both anticipation and fear. She couldn't help but fear that it would disappoint her when she stepped inside. Not because of Daniel's craftsmanship, but of not having her mother by her side.

"What do you want to show me?" Celia asked when they stopped by the gate of her new yard.

"Go inside and see for yourself," Sarah encouraged her with a bright smile.

Lucas handed her a set of keys and hugged her tightly. "We really hope you like it."

Celia wasn't sure if she could do this. Especially not alone. As if sensing her hesitation, Lucas opened the gate for her. "We'll be right here if you need us."

Celia drew in a deep breath and walked through the garden gate. She made her way on the pathway she hadn't noticed towards the porch and stopped at the foot of the steps. She glanced back towards Lucas and Sarah and saw them gesturing her to go inside.

Step by step, she ascended the stairs, stopping for a moment to admire the spacious porch. She could furnish it with rocking chairs and a porch swing if she wanted. Perhaps a few flower boxes…

The light of a lantern caught her eye through the glass of the front door. Celia turned towards it and slowly turned the nob.

The scent of lumber, varnish, and lemon oil flooded her senses as she opened the door. The open living area was exactly how she envisioned it to be in her mind. But in her mind, she never imagined Daniel standing in the dining room waiting for her.

"Daniel?" Celia asked, pleasantly surprised.

"I'm your surprise," Daniel announced happily.

Laughter bubbled from Celia's throat. "I thought the haus was my surprise."

"That too," Daniel shrugged. "Kumm, let me show you."

Celia stopped counting the number of times she caught her breath as Daniel took her through her new home. Every single surface had been sanded to a fine sheen. The closets, built-in, in the bedrooms, were spacious and had beautifully carved doors.

After mentioning she might use the mudroom as a sunroom in winter, Daniel had added more windows and a see-through roof to allow more light into the space. If Celia could've dreamed of having the perfect home, then she wouldn't have been able to imagine it as perfect as the one she stood in now.

Daniel had decided that now that it was only Celia, it would be better for her to have the master bedroom to the left instead of the rooms with the shared bathroom. He left the master suite until the very last.

He opened the door and the first thing that caught Celia's eye was the beautiful bed. It had hand carved posts, matching side tables and a dreamy mosquito net hanging over it from the roof.

"Daniel, this is…" Celia shook her head, not finding the words to express her feelings.

Daniel pulled away the mosquito net and revealed the quilt on the bed. "Daisy and Lucas insisted."

Celia's throat clogged with emotion. On her bed lay the very last bed spread her mother and father had ever shared. One that her mother had quilted with Celia's help, sewn by hand and cared for with love.

It hadn't been used since the day they had buried her father.

Daniel lay a hand on her shoulder. "They knew how much it meant to you."

Celia nodded, struggling to find the words.

As if understanding, Daniel led her back to the spacious living room. She still needed couches and a few more items of furniture, but she hadn't even noticed the dining table in the dining room when she had stepped inside. "But that's Lucas's?"

Daniel shook his head. "Lucas inherited most of your parents' furniture. Daisy only asked for your mamm's bed and her hope chest. Lucas insisted that the reason there was so much laughter and love around this table in the last few years is because you made sure of it. This is a welcome home gift from your siblings."

Celia turned to him with tears in her eyes. "I'm so blessed, Daniel. But the bed... where did that come from?"

Daniel pulled out a chair and Celia took a seat. He reached for her hand and searched her gaze. "I made it for you."

The gesture was so much more than the gesture of a friend, so much more intimate, but Celia wasn't ready to become hopeful just yet. Instead, she smiled and brushed away a tear. "Denke, I'll cherish it, always."

With Lucas and Ryan's help, Daniel had finished Celia's home a few days ahead of time. He'd made certain that their secret remained just that, wanting to surprise Celia when everything was ready.

Just two days ago, he'd spoken to Lucas and revealed his feelings for Celia. Although Celia was a grown woman, it only felt right to ask for Lucas's permission to court her. But now that she was here, right before him and everything was as he hoped it would be, Daniel found himself at a loss for words.

He had planned tonight with such care, wanting everything to be perfect, only to realize nothing had been perfect until now.

This house had become a home the moment Celia had stepped inside. Instead of the scent of new lumber, he could smell the lavender water on her skin, and the scent of flowers in her shampoo. His heart swelled with love, wondering how he could ever put those emotions into words.

Daniel took a deep breath and searched Celia's eyes, praying that he would find the word. "Celia, when I started on this project, I didn't think it would differ from any other project. But on that very first day I came by, I knew it would be different." Daniel knew he might drag it out, but he wanted Celia to understand how his feelings for her had developed and how deep they had become. "I wanted to build the perfect home, just because I knew you were going to live in it."

"Ach, Daniel…" Celia sighed with a smile.

Daniel shook his head. "Let me finish. At first, I think it was curiosity, because you had become almost a hermit over the last few years. But as I came to work every day, I realized it was so much more than that. I came to look forward to seeing you, to getting to know you, to spending time with you. And before I knew it, I fell head over heels in love with you."

Celia wiped away a tear, but Daniel wasn't finished just yet.

"I fell in love with your smile, with your optimism, with the way you cared for your mother, and the way you never once complained. I fell in love with your selflessness, with your heart and your beautiful soul. I knew that the time wasn't right, so I didn't act on it. Instead, I stole your time whenever I had a chance. Just enough to make me fall a little deeper in love every time." Daniel searched her gaze and saw his feelings reflected in her gaze. "But when you lost your mamm... I knew you needed time. You needed to find yourself and I needed to make sure that when you did your haus would be waiting for you to start your new life."

"You think I'm ready to start my new life?" Celia asked, evidently doubting herself.

Daniel nodded. "I know you haven't shared your feelings with me, but if I'm right, you feel the same way?"

"I do," Celia agreed. "I was afraid at first, and when Mamm passed, I was so lost. I think I would've still been lost if you hadn't chastened me that day on the porch for not taking care of myself. I was so angry with you... but now I'm grateful because you were right. And you were there. This entire time you've been there for me, I don't know how I can ever show you how grateful I am for that."

Daniel stood up with a mysterious smile and got down on one knee. He reached for Celia's hand and smiled up at her with hope shining in his gaze. "I can ask you to allow me to court you, but I don't want to waste another day of my life knowing you're not mine to love and to care for. Start your new life with me Celia, be my frau. Let me stand by your side for the rest of your life and let me share this home with you. I want to you to be the mamm of my kinner, I want you to be the frau I fall asleep with every night and the one I wake up to every morning. Will you marry me?"

For a moment Daniel thought he'd overplayed his hand when Celia's eyes grew wide with surprise or horror. He wasn't sure which.

But his doubt only lasted a second before a smile split her face in two and she cried out with joy.

"Jah!"

Epilogue

"Mamm would've been so happy," Daisy said, taking Celia's hand as they walked from Celia's new home to the barn.

"I like to think so," Celia said with a smile.

Children raced past tables laden heavy with food and drink as the entire community mulled between the barn and the two houses. Buggies lined the dirt road for as far as the eye could see. The only sign that this wasn't an ordinary picnic or a birthday celebration was the bride's table that stood by the entrance of the barn.

Daisy laughed as they reached the table. "I still can't believe we planned a wedding in just two weeks."

Celia chuckled. "I know. It's hard to believe myself. But we did, and it's perfect."

"Just like Mamm taught us. I even remembered to iron the tablecloths," Daisy teased.

Celia glanced around at the people she had known since childhood. Some old, some young, some the age her parents would've been today. Instead of feeling bereft for not having them there, she was grateful that they had given her this.

They had given her a home, a community that cared, and siblings that would always love her regardless of the fact they weren't family by birth.

"A beautiful wedding for my favorite schweschder," Lucas teased as he joined them.

Daisy playfully slapped his arm. The teasing had begun the moment Daisy had seen Celia's home. It was good natured, in every sense.

"Denke for everything. You're my favorite bruder," Celia said, pressing a kiss to his cheek. It was still strange seeing Lucas with the beard he had grown after his wedding. Soon, Daniel would have one as well, she reminded herself.

She might not wear a ring to show her commitment, but the color of her new prayer kapp would show it, just like Daniel's beard would show his marital status.

"Do you think Mamm and Daed ever imagined all of us living on this farm?" Lucas asked, glancing first at Daisy's cottage in the distance before he turned to his own home and Celia's new house.

"Nee, but I think it would please them to know that we're all still together. Close enough to help and care, but far enough to lead our own lives," Daisy offered her opinion.

"I agree. And close enough for me to babysit whenever you need it," Celia said, stroking her sister's belly.

Daisy glanced at Sarah and let out a sigh. "I still have four months to go. She's lucky it's almost over."

"Never wish away time," Celia said almost at the same time as her brother. It was something their mother had said when they were children, and now meant so much more to them after losing her.

"I'm not," Daisy said simply. "I'm going to find some more food; I swear it seems as if my stomach has become an endless pit of hunger."

Celia and Lucas laughed as Daisy walked away. Lucas turned to Celia with a loving smile and shook his head. "You're the glue, you know?"

"The glue?" Celia asked, confused.

"The glue that kept our familye together. When Mamm got sick, when Daisy was confused about her adoption, right till the end, you were the glue. Even now," Lucas explained.

Celia laughed. "And soon the new babies will take that position."

"Soon," Lucas agreed. "I better go check on Sarah, make sure she plated for me."

Celia watched her brother walk towards his wife even as Daniel approached her with a slice of cake. "Would you like a piece of wedding cake, Mrs. Stoltzfus?"

Celia laughed. "Mrs. Stoltzfus, that makes me sound old."

"Nee, it makes you sound like my frau. Taste it; I swear this is the best cake I've ever tasted," Daniel insisted, holding a piece up for Celia to bite.

Celia swallowed, pleased with the flavor and texture. "You're right, it is gut."

"Find out about this recipe. I'll love you forever if you bake it for me," Daniel said before taking another bite.

"I thought you already promised to love me forever?" Celia teased. "You're in luck. It's my recipe."

Daniel's eyes smiled with pleasure. "See, I knew I picked the right frau."

"I still can't believe we're married," Celia said, shaking her head.

Daniel chuckled. "The bishop says we're the Amish example of an Englisch shotgun wedding. No hesitation, no planning, just jumping right onto the wild horse without fear."

"Are you afraid?" Celia asked a little more seriously.

Daniel shook his head. "Nee, not even the faintest bit. I know Gott planned for us to be together. With you by my side and Gott in my heart, what do I have to fear?"

Celia's smile softened. "Daniel, you're gut for my soul, you know that?"

"You're not gut for my waistline," Daniel teased, taking another bite of the cake.

A commotion on the other side of the gathering caught their eye. Both Daniel and Celia moved towards the people, parting away from something. There, right by the refreshment table, Sarah stood, looking completely horrified.

"Sarah?" Lucas asked, quiet enough only for Sarah and Celia to hear. "Did you have an accident here? In front of all these people?"

Before Sarah could answer, Celia laughed. "She did no such thing, you ferhoodled fool. She's in labor. Her water just broke."

"What!" Lucas cried out as if she'd just announced there was a tsunami on its way to Lancaster County.

"She's about to have your boppli. Could you please try to calm down and call the midwife?" Celia asked as she helped Sarah towards her house.

When Celia turned to look if the men had moved, she couldn't help but laugh. "I thought you weren't afraid of anything?"

Daniel cleared his throat and shook his head. "Except this. We're terrified of this."

"Gut, it's a good thing you're not needed then. Find the midwife and send her in. We're about to have an Eymann baby," Celia announced.

As soon as the words left her mouth, she saw both Lucas and Daisy looking at her with a smile. They might have been adopted, but the baby that was about to be born would be a true Eymann.

Their familye by heart and soul, because at the end of the day that's more important than any blood.

*** The End ***

Thank you kindly for choosing to read my book. I sincerely hope you enjoyed it. All of my Amish Romances are wholesome stories suitable for all to enjoy.

If you could be so kind to leave a review on Amazon, I would appreciate it.